A VIRTUOSO PERFORMANCE
. . . IN MURDER

Beth swung in through the door of the studio. I followed.

"There's our hero," she said, quickening her step. "Napping on the job. Nowhere near the piano."

Will Gryder was seated in an armchair in a space in the barn cut off from the rest of the studio by two antique sofas placed at right angles to each other.

"Willy, I want you to meet my . . ."

The introduction became garbled. Beth turned toward me and her eyes were huge, terrible.

Then she was screaming. Clawing at me as she fell forward.

I tried to right her, hold her up, looking over to the quiet man in the chair for help.

He could offer no help. A sharp object with a wooden handle had been driven deep into the center of his chest. The flannel shirt he was wearing was drenched with blood. Blood. Blood. Blood.

A CAT WITH A FIDDLE

An Alice Nestleton Mystery

by

Lydia Adamson

A SIGNET BOOK

SIGNET
Published by the Penguin Group
Penguin Books USA Inc., 375 Hudson Street,
New York, New York 10014, U.S.A.
Penguin Books Ltd, 27 Wrights Lane, London W8 5TZ, England
Penguin Books Australia Ltd, Ringwood, Victoria, Australia
Penguin Books Canada Ltd, 10 Alcorn Avenue,
Toronto, Ontario, Canada M4V 3B2
Penguin Books (N.Z.) Ltd, 182-190 Wairau Road, Auckland 10, New Zealand

Penguin Books Ltd, Registered Offices:
Harmondsworth, Middlesex, England

First published by Signet, an imprint of New American Library,
a division of Penguin Books USA Inc.

First Printing, May, 1993
10 9 8 7 6 5 4 3 2 1

The first chapter of this book previously appeared in *A Cat in the Wings*.

 REGISTERED TRADEMARK—MARCA REGISTRADA

Printed in the United States of America

PUBLISHER'S NOTE
This is a work of fiction. Names, characters, places, and incidents either are the product of the author's imagination or are used fictitiously, and any resemblance to actual persons, living or dead, events, or locales is entirely coincidental.

A CAT WITH
A FIDDLE

1

I know an actor who was born on the Lower East Side of New York City. Jerry has always said that the single scariest thing he could ever imagine was being alone on a dark night in the country. As someone born and bred on a farm, I've always laughed at his city paranoia.

But that autumn night, lost in rural Massachusetts, I understood what Jerry meant. The darkness seemed to double every few minutes, and there was nothing I could do to hold it back.

I couldn't figure out which switch on the panel of knobs in my rented car was for the brights. And to make matters worse, Lulu was clawing at my ankles, down near the accelerator. I hadn't attached the clasp on the cat-carrier securely enough, and she'd escaped from the box.

Of course Lulu wasn't my cat. Mine were safe at home, being watched over alternately by my friend Tony and my neighbor Mrs. Oshrin. Lulu was a brown tabby Scottish Fold with knockout gold eyes and the sweetest ears on earth—they folded down over themselves. She was my cat-sitting charge and she lived ordinarily with Beth Stimson, a woman about my age, the second violinist with the Riverside String Quartet. Beth had asked me to pack up Lulu and bring her up

to western Mass., where she was vacationing—or "retreating," as she'd described it—for a
few weeks. The place where she was staying,
Beth said, was overrun with field mice, and
Lulu's talents as a hunter were needed. I knew
better, though. I knew she was just lonely for her
kitty.

But when she proposed that I turn the trip up
there into a little holiday for myself, why did I
agree to it so eagerly? I needed a break, is why,
a vacation. I needed it bad. Not only had the
play I'd been starring in way off-Broadway
closed ignominiously after eleven performances,
but my performance had been singled out and
roundly panned. Not just panned. Excoriated.
By a very well known guest drama critic writing
in *The New Yorker*.

He had said, among other things:

Alice Nestleton has a deserved reputation as
one of the best underappreciated actresses in
the American theater, but this performance
does nothing to mitigate her dilemma.

Granted, it is very difficult to translate
Henry James onto the stage (though some
brilliant exceptions prove this rule). Granted
that James's *Beast in the Jungle* is one of the
most perplexing of his later works, being a
story of two people caught in an opaque ob-
session that prevents them from consum-
mating their love. All this aside, Miss
Nestleton's claustrophobic, motherly por-
trayal of the doomed heroine May Bartam is
deadly, and the most wrong-headed inter-
pretation of a major role this reviewer has
witnessed in many a season.

I had managed to cope. Friends had been most supportive. But I needed a vacation.

Obviously I'd missed a turnoff somewhere, or misread a road sign. The tall trees overhanging the road from both sides seemed to pursue me on this drive to nowhere. And now Lulu was *really* misbehaving.

I pulled over onto a shoulder of the road and got her back inside the carrier. I fumbled around until I could locate the overhead lights and then consulted the maps of the area that Tony had purchased for me at the travel book store near Rockefeller Center.

It was turning cold, and I could feel the wind slicing through the little compact. But as I studied the map, I began to feel a little better about my situation. If the small white sign telling me that I was just entering the hamlet of Hopewell was to be believed, I wasn't really so very lost. All I had to do was focus on getting to Northampton—which apparently I had overshot by a few miles. Beth Stimson had in fact mentioned Northampton to me before I set out. She was staying at a place called Covington Center—whatever that was—which was on the outskirts of a small village called Covington, which in turn was a forty-minute drive from the larger entity of Northampton.

Now, Northampton I knew because it was the home of Smith College, where I'd not only attended a workshop once but been guest lecturer to a group of drama students—through the good graces of my friend Amanda Avery, who was a professor in the drama department.

I thought of that saying, "You can't get there from here." In other words, I was lost because I was trying to find Covington, and the only way to get to Covington was to first find Northampton. So I did.

It was nearly ten when I made the sharp turn off the road onto the grounds of the place. It turned out to be neither a hotel nor a bed-and-breakfast nor a precious New England inn. The roughly weathered sign on a post at the entrance read: COVINGTON CENTER FOR THE ARTS. ESTABLISHED 1919.

There was a huge main house, with lights burning. I could see only the outlines of the darkened smaller buildings behind it. I drove slowly up to the house, parked on what had once been a lawn, grabbed the cat, and started toward the door.

"Where do you think you're going?"

I turned, startled by the voice, and found myself staring at a weary-looking woman about to deposit a plastic garbage bag in a large wooden receptacle at the side of the house.

"I'm looking for Beth Stimson," I answered rather gruffly, matching the woman's tone.

"Oh. Well, go in," she said impatiently. "Don't just stand there—go in."

I knocked loudly and then opened the heavy door. Coming to meet me was Beth, her long brown hair pulled away from her face and spilling down the back of a black turtleneck sweater.

"Here you are!" she called out. "I was worried about you—just about to call for the Mounties."

"I just got a little lost, Beth." I stooped to undo the clasp on the carrier, and Lulu and friend were reunited.

I heard music from somewhere inside the house. Schubert. I looked past Beth and Lulu, through the dark parlor all the way to the enormous kitchen. I could see a corner of a great oak table, at which another woman sat holding a drink. There were others back there, too. I could hear the low rumble of their voices.

"Come this way, Alice." Beth had let Lulu out of her arms and was now taking hold of my elbow. "I'll introduce you to the guys."

The "guys" weren't really guys. They were three lovely women, Beth's associates in the Riverside String Quartet. I was presented, one by one, to Roz Polikoff, first violinist; Darcy Wilson, the violist, and Miranda Bly, cellist. Also in attendance was Mathew Hazan, the cherubic manager of the group, and Ben Polikoff, whose face I recognized from the newspapers, because he was a powerful New York businessman.

When Beth had invited me up for a respite, it hadn't even occurred to me that her entire group would also be in residence. I wondered what kind of vacation she was having, and what kind I'd have. Of course I'd heard of all the women in the group, though I might not have been able to name them individually. After all, the Riverside was one of the first successful all-women classical groups; they had been around for quite a while, since the late 1970s. They were all, in a sense, celebrities.

"And this is our cook, Mrs. Wallace," Beth said, gesturing toward the tart woman who had accosted me outside. Mrs. Wallace had a better opportunity to run her appraising eye over me in the light. She nodded curtly and withdrew. I had apparently come in in the middle of a party—or perhaps a brainstorming session—or maybe they were all just relaxing after a late dinner. At any rate, the table was a riot of cheese rinds and fruit peelings and dessert plates and coffee mugs, and there was a giant bottle of Martell cognac in the middle of it all.

Darcy Wilson, who was black and petite and extremely pretty, picked up Lulu and began to inspect her. "She doesn't look like the champion mouser of North America to me, Beth."

"Have faith," Beth answered lightly, and it was only then that I remembered the ostensible reason for Lulu's presence in the house.

"We have another hand around here, Alice," Beth said. "But he appears not to be on deck at the moment. Where *is* dear Will, anyway?"

"Probably off somewhere admiring his own reflection." It was Miranda, the cellist, who had spoken. She lit a cigarette.

The cryptic reference, I learned a minute later, was to Will Gryder, the concert pianist who often appeared as guest soloist with the quartet. That was Will, Roz Polikoff informed me, playing Schubert. An old performance of his had just been resurrected and issued on compact disc.

"You know Will," Mathew Hazan said, chuckling. "He's probably in the studio brooding."

"Well, I'm going to show Alice around a little," Beth said, steering me toward the kitchen door that led outside.

"Come back for a drink, Alice!" Ben called.

"I will, thanks."

"Carry on, children," Beth said. But before we left, she pulled a beautifully worn sheepskin coat off a hook near the pantry. "You'll need this," she said, handing it to me. "You're not dressed warmly enough."

She was right. It had grown colder. But it was

a beautiful night, the stars all around. "You can see more tomorrow," Beth said. "In the light. This is a wonderful place. Let's walk up the hill, okay? I'll introduce you to Will."

"Fine," I said. "What is this place, Beth? A religious retreat or something like that?"

"Hardly. It's a working artist colony. You know, painters and writers and sculptors and composers and so on—a lot of them on grants. But money's tight now. They only operate in the spring and summer and the rest of the year they rent it out, month by month, to private groups."

We walked slowly uphill in the black night, rocks crunching under our feet. She was sure-footed in the dark, never once glancing over, as I did from time to time, at the rustling woods surrounding us.

"You're probably wondering what we're all doing up here," she said after a minute.

"I assume you're practicing—or whatever."

"Not exactly. At least, not *just* that."

There was something elliptical about the remark. I waited for her to continue.

"Being up here is . . . oh, kind of a remedy . . . a recuperation for us . . . after that European tour. Which was, in a word, awful. It was a real disaster. We played abominably. We fought. We were almost crucified by the critics. And we came back just beaten and exhausted. They said we had lost it, Alice. That we might be four good musicians, but nothing resembling a quartet. Not a single entity. It hurts when you get notices like that. It really hurts."

"Oh," I said, "I think I know what it feels like."

"Hmm. But the sad thing is, who could argue

with them? We were just burned out, I guess. So when we got back, Mat said it was to time to regroup—no pun intended. He thought it would be good for us to get away, away from all pressure, rethink what we're going to be about next season, perfect some things that have just kind of gotten away from us. But more important, he wants us to just get to know each other again, get back in touch with how much we all . . . need . . . love each other. So he rented this heavenly place and got us a cook to stuff us with good food. We were just supposed to do an old-fashioned retreat—no husbands, no lovers, no— well, no pets. We're just supposed to talk and play and relax. But as you can see, little by little we're bringing our city lives up here. One item at a time."

Beth stopped explaining the situation then, and began to point out the overgrown paths to the various cabins and studios on the property. I heard a brook somewhere in the woods, running back down the hill.

We could see the outline of Will's studio in the moonlight. It was a large converted barn, with dormered windows running all around the second story.

Beth picked up the thread of the previous topic. "I guess this *was* supposed to be a spiritual retreat, in a way. But I don't know if it's working. Maybe we're too old, too cynical. Anyway, like I said, one item at a time. First Roz's husband Ben—but that was to be expected, I suppose. Roz is a genius at getting what she wants."

I held in my mind the image of the pale-skinned violinist Roz: a magnificent mane of impossibly curly strawberry-blond hair, impossibly piercing blue eyes, a perfect, hungry mouth with impossibly perfect teeth, a voice exactly the one you wish could sing you to sleep at night.

"Then Will shows up," Beth went on, "then Lulu. Darcy'll probably ask her sister's kid up next week. Oh, well . . . I guess nothing ever works out exactly as planned, does it? Except maybe Bach."

We were standing on the grass outside the barn by then. "Are you sure Will won't mind being disturbed?" I asked. "Perhaps he wants to brood alone."

Beth laughed. "I doubt that. I've never known Will to pass up an opportunity to meet a beautiful woman. And vice versa, pretty much."

She swung in through the door of the studio. I followed. The interior was breathtaking with its high vaulted ceiling, from which hung enormous, rich tapestries. The indirect lights, hidden behind ceiling lanterns, were invisible from outside, but inside they lit the huge space with glancing beams.

"There's our hero," she said, quickening her step. "Napping on the job. And nowhere near the piano."

Gryder was seated in an armchair, in that space in the barn cut off from the rest of the studio by two antique sofas placed at right angles to each other.

"Willy, I want you to meet my. . . ."

The introduction became garbled. Beth turned toward me and her eyes were huge, terrible.

Then she was screaming. Clawing at me as she fell forward.

I tried to right her, hold her up, looking over to the quiet man in the chair for help.

He could offer no help. A sharp object with a wooden handle had been driven deep into the center of his chest. The flannel shirt he was wearing was drenched with blood. Blood. Blood. Blood.

2

Situations like that are really weird. Once the shock and panic and the hysterical running around are done—once the police come and impose a kind of clinical order on things—the time begins to crawl.

My legs had grown stiff.

It was a real effort not to keep looking at the old clock on the mantel. This was a solemn affair, after all, and constantly monitoring the time would be like checking your watch at a funeral. Finally I did go over for a look, though, only to realize the clock wasn't working.

But I knew it must be at least two in the morning.

The tall, strong-jawed state policeman in charge of the case had introduced himself as "Lieutenant Donaldson." That had been ages ago. He and his men had since methodically peeled back and pried into and turned up every inch of the murder site and the main house and fanned out onto the darkened grounds.

Now I was sitting with Beth and her colleagues in the manorly living room of the old house. As we waited for further instructions—if not orders—from the police, once in a while someone would voice his sorrow or express impatience with the goings-on. But for the most part we were silent, waiting out the dragging minutes.

I felt very much the intruder. Perhaps it was because I had always stood in awe of classical musicians, and these women were world-class. My grandmother had instilled that awe in me. As was true for many isolated rural people, the weekly radio concerts and the old seventy-eight records she'd collected had been profoundly liberating for her. I remember well the absolute joy on Gram's face as she listened to her favorite scratchy record: the London String Quartet playing the Brahms Opus 67. And I remember how she used to handle that boxed edition of the complete Beethoven quartets played by the Budapest String Quartet. She'd stand holding the box, staring at it before removing one of the discs, as if they contained a gospel.

I found myself idly wondering what commanding officer Donaldson's first name was. I knew I was being silly, but it was as good a way as any to pass the time. He looked like a Lewis, I decided, or possibly a Calvin—or even a strange, singular kind of Pete.

Miranda Bly came back into the room, released from her session with the lieutenant, just as I was turning over the name *Aloyisius* Donaldson in my mind. I guess the lieutenant was finished with her—for now.

Miranda headed straight for the armchair where she'd left her cigarettes. She sat down wordlessly and lit up.

Then Mrs. Wallace brought in that huge bottle of cognac. We all fell upon it. Thank God, she had softened toward me a little; she'd offered an hour ago to make me a cheese-and-tomato sandwich (she'd baked the bread just that morning, she told me, as though I really cared at that point) and had brought with it a hunk of homemade spice cake and a glass of delicious cider. I had had nothing to eat since lunch back in New York.

Darcy had been snuffling quietly for the last hour or so, fidgeting in her seat. But now she rose and went over to poke the fire. She moved with great economy, as if she had once been a dancer. Beth got up and joined her. I could see her speaking to Darcy, but I couldn't hear her words.

Ben Polikoff, wearing an expensive red ski sweater, filled his wife's brandy snifter yet again. He was trying to comfort Roz, obviously, but she seemed to be in another dimension. She was staring straight ahead into what under other circumstances would have been a very cozy fire; she was plainly somewhere else, disconnected from the rest of us. Her skin was a ghostly white, her eyes milky. Roz was even more beautiful in her grief—or shock, or loss, or whatever had seized her. I saw her shrug off her husband's comforting arm absentmindedly. Ben looked over helplessly at Miranda, who glanced away.

Mrs. Wallace reappeared then, coffee pot in hand. I saw the strain in her face as she bent to fill each of our cups.

"Thank you," I said when it was my turn. "Can you tell how far along they are out there?" By that, I meant Donaldson and his men.

"None of my affair," she replied immediately.

"But if you think *you* can hurry those stupid cops along ... well, more power to you."

But I didn't have long to wait for a real answer to my question. Mathew Hazan came in shortly, looking shaken but resolute. He kept compulsively tidying his longish black hair. In his gray shirt and gray corduroy suit, he looked very much like a professor at some prestigious university—like Wesleyan—who has just delivered a lecture on ambiguity in Haydn's middle period.

And with Hazan's entrance we were all back together again. Donaldson had now interviewed each of us in the dusty library next to the sitting room.

Soon the lieutenant made an entrance of his own. He certainly was crisp for three in the morning—lightly graying hair all in place, Ivy League pink shirt nice and starched under his wool sport coat, trousers demonically pleated ... I wondered whether he'd taken the time to shave as well.

Donaldson stood surveying the room, sizing us up before he spoke. There was a hint of Gary Cooper—the *High Noon* incarnation—in his stance. I watched his Adam's apple intently as he began to talk.

"It'll be just a while longer before you folks can get to bed," he started. Firm but polite, but not deferential. "I have some preliminary information I can give you all now, but of course we'll have to wait for the coroner's report before anything's official.

"Looks to me as though Mr. Gryder died around eight tonight. But like I said, that isn't gospel. The apparent cause of death was a blow struck into the victim's . . . into Mr. Gryder's chest with a chisel. The weapon is the sort of thing a sculptor would use. Now, that's in keeping with the kind of tool used by some of the artists that would've stayed in the barn where Mr. Gryder had his studio.

"We found no signs of a struggle. It seems Mr. Gryder was seated—relaxed, so to speak—when he was killed. This means there's a very good possibility he knew the attacker." Donaldson paused here, displaying not a bad sense of drama, and looked fleetingly from face to face.

"But on the other hand, a search of his room here in the house didn't turn up his wallet or any of the jewelry he was said to be wearing. So naturally robbery is a strong possibility.

"There have been two reported instances of theft or vandalism here at the school in the last year, but—"

"Actually this isn't a school, Lieutenant Donaldson." It was Mat Hazan who spoke. "It's a colony for artists."

Donaldson turned grimly alert eyes on Hazan. He waited a few moments before resuming. "The two incidents over the past year were not particularly serious. But in each case they entered the school property on foot. Now, as you folks know, we've had a bit of a frost up here. The ground is too packed to show much of anything. So we're pretty much out of luck as far as footprints go.

"Whoever killed Mr. Gryder was careful with the weapon as well. We haven't—"

In the doorway, one of Donaldson's uniformed underlings, a small-built man, had suddenly appeared. "Ford?" he called. "See you out here? Just a sec."

So my silly game about his first name was over. I had my answer. *Ford* Donaldson. Nice and stoic. Very American. Like John Ford. Or Ford Maddox Ford, who wrote *The Good Soldier.* No doubt Ford Donaldson was a good soldier, too.

He stepped out of the room to consult with his man. And for the first time since the patrol cars had raced up the driveway, this cultivated group of friends, family and colleagues became animated.

"What an officious, self-important prick he is!" Miranda spat out. "I suppose he thinks we're impressed with his pathetic Clint Eastwood act."

I was a bit startled by her angry response to Donaldson. But then again, I had dealt with many NYPD detectives who made Donaldson sound like a vice-president in a public relations firm. And Miranda, most likely, had not.

Benjamin Polikoff had begun a bit of circular pacing. "Oh, he's out to impress, all right," he said. "There's no doubt of that. Put the city slickers in their place. If those are his priorities I—" Someone in the room laughed at the use of the word "priorities," but Polikoff continued unfazed. "If those are his priorities, I don't know how much confidence we should place in his investigation."

"There must be some other authority we can call," Mathew Hazan said hopefully. "The FBI or something. I have to wonder whether the local people up here have the . . . the equipment for dealing with a thing like this."

"The equipment, or the brains?" I asked quietly.

"Don't misunderstand, Miss Nestleton. I meant no insult to the Massachusetts State Police as a group, or any of the gentlemen on the premises. But you must understand, it's as if a family member had been killed. Will Gryder was important to each and every one of us—extremely important. Not to mention his importance to the cultural life of New York—and the world."

That has to be an exaggeration, I thought. Not that I fancied myself among the classical music cognoscente, but I knew very well that Gryder had hardly been a household word. Horowitz, perhaps, but not Gryder.

"I just want to see to it that something is done!" Hazan continued.

"Of course we want to see something *done*, Mathew," Beth Stimson said. "But what's the point of you and Ben throwing your weight around? What's it going to do but alienate this man Donaldson further?"

I made sure to modulate my voice. I wanted to be careful not to step on anyone's toes, do any alienating of my own. "Actually," I said, "Lieutenant Donaldson may be a little high-handed, but from what they've let us see, he seems very competent. And while he may not see the range of crimes a New York policeman might, the standards for state policemen—especially homicide detectives—are probably even higher than in the city. In fact, the training probably comes closer to FBI standards than the average big-city cop's does." *Now, why am I pontificating this way?*

Miranda snorted. "Oh, I see. The situation's in

hand. Then I suppose we can sit back and relax—like Will did. I'd forgotten, Beeswax," she said, turning to Beth Stimson. "You told us your cat person was also an armchair criminologist. Right, Miss Nestleton?"

"Well, yes," I said pleasantly. "Armchair. Amateur. Whatever. But, frankly, I'd never counsel anyone to sit back and relax when there might be a murderer nearby. . . . And please, call me Alice," I said. Then I addressed them en masse. "All of you, please just call me Alice. I know I'm not really a part of your group, but we may all be spending a great deal of time together."

Darcy, with an amused look on her face, sauntered over to me. "A little more brandy, Alice?" she asked. And when I held up my glass, she said, "Please explain about the time we're all going to be spending together."

But the lieutenant returned at that moment.

"As I was saying, the chisel used to kill Mr. Gryder was wiped down. One thing we can say about this killer: He—or she—had a lot of time to cover his tracks, clean things up. I'm wondering if it was common for Mr. Gryder to spend so much time away from the rest of you people. According to your statements, he left the dinner table very early, maybe even a little abruptly. Not very sociable, was he? Or was that just last night?"

Mathew Hazan answered first. "Will was here to work. If the urge to work occurs at dinnertime, then it comes at dinnertime. No one minded that he left."

"But he was working with you, if I understand it."

"Not solely. Will appears—appeared—with

the Riverside Quartet, but as a guest artist. He wasn't a member of the group. He said he was working on a new composition."

"So he wrote music too?"

"And he was a studio musician," Beth cut in. "And a voice coach sometimes. Will did a variety of things."

"Some better than others," Miranda added, barely audibly. Audibly enough for there to be a hint of threat—or something else—in her words.

Roz Polikoff came to life then. "Jesus, Miranda, will you *stop* that—please! Just stop it!"

Donaldson waited out the silence that fell over the room. All eyes were on Roz, who looked in Miranda's direction pleadingly.

"If you're playing the bitch to cover up how frightened you are, you can just drop it," Roz said hoarsely, a catch in her voice. "You're making this man think something's wrong here, that we didn't all . . . love Willy."

"We're making him think a lot more than that," Darcy mumbled. "Just take it easy, Miran. C'mon, give us a cigarette. Even though I've quit."

I saw the wetness shimmering on Miranda's eyelashes as she passed over the pack.

Ben handed Roz his handkerchief. "Look, Lieutenant Donaldson, can't I please take my wife to bed now?"

Darcy exploded with laughter at Ben's awkwardly phrased request. She grabbed her mouth as if attempting to push the laughs back in. Everyone, I realized, was becoming unhinged.

"Oh, God," said Darcy. "Sorry, everybody. Sorry."

"This is grotesque," Miranda said.

"I said I'd let you go soon," Donaldson assured us. "And I will. Just tell me, which one of you would have the address and phone number of Carolyn Bakiris?"

"Who's Carolyn Bakiris?" Ben asked.

"Will's sister," Mat said with a sigh. "She's married, living out in LA. I have it. It's in my book—upstairs."

"But shouldn't one of us tell her?" Beth said. "It's going to be so awful to hear it from some—" She broke off and looked guiltily over at Donaldson. "I mean, it should be one of his friends who gives her the news."

"And why should that be you?" Predictably, it was Miranda who spoke, but there was little venom in the question.

"*I'll* speak to his sister," Hazan said firmly. "When Lieutenant Donaldson here gives me permission to do so, that is."

"One of my men will go with you to your room for the number," Donaldson said, ignoring the edge in Mathew's voice. "I think," he added, turning to us, "that about does it for now. Except for one last thing."

Mathew stopped in the doorway. Miranda straightened in her chair. Ben paused momentarily in helping Roz from hers. Darcy placed the disposable lighter down silently on the cigarette table. Beth breathed noisily.

"I'm asking that you all remain here while this investigation proceeds."

"Are we to understand we're under some sort of house arrest?" Ben asked incredulously.

"No," Donaldson said. "Of course not. It

wouldn't be legal—even if that's what I wanted to do. I mean, remain in the area. Available."

"Will may be dead, Lieutenant. But our work goes on. We'll remain for the rest of our lease here—another two weeks."

The officer said nothing. Once again, he swept those searchlight eyes of his across our faces. He focused on me a few seconds longer than the situation warranted, I thought, but I didn't look away.

I wondered if this man was carrying a knapsack of pain on his back. And telling himself it didn't hurt at all. That he'd just have to walk straighter. What was it—a recent divorce? A promotion that had never materialized? A case he'd never solved? Illness? Impotence? Alcohol?

My theater training was beginning to get the better of me. Interpret the role. Study the character. Look for the hidden biographical strands. Feel the character's past traumas. Construct the role from the bottom up. Don't look at the face— look at the lines in it.

By the time I'd pursued all those strands, Ford Donaldson was saying good night to us. I caught the tail end of something about his being "sorry for everyone's loss." He also informed us that one of his men would be remaining on the premises.

"You don't mean you think he . . . they . . . might come back?" Beth asked in alarm.

"*Is* that what you're saying, Lieutenant Donaldson?" Ben demanded to know.

"What I'm saying is, we're not taking any chance of that happening," Donaldson replied.

Then, just as he was turning to go, Lulu, with her divine ears, appeared out of nowhere.

And Donaldson, after first stepping on her tail, which sent her yowling under the sofa, exited hopping and stumbling into the night.

As the door slammed shut, Darcy said tartly, "He's a piece of work, isn't he?"

We didn't go to bed right away, as late as it was. Except for Roz. I'm not certain that she was quite as exhausted as Ben thought, but she seemed to grow weary all over again at his solicitude. In the end she allowed him to see her upstairs, leaving the rest of the group gathered around the dying fire.

I knew I was now, more than ever, the interloper in the crowd. I couldn't join in the reminiscences of Will. But my native curiosity overrode any hurt I might have felt at being excluded from the talk. I sat quietly and listened.

"God, what a horror," Miranda said. "I keep thinking it's time for someone to pinch me and wake me up. . . . Willy, Willy, how did this happen?"

"I bet he's mad as hell he won't get to do that Berlin gig," Darcy said, smiling and crying at the same time.

"Yes," Mathew agreed. "That was Willy— always narrowly missing it. So talented, and stretched so thin, and yet . . . oh, I don't know . . . it's as if he spent his life missing trains."

"Willy was very careless, wasn't he?" Beth said quietly.

"What is that supposed to mean?" Miranda spoke.

"I mean, sure he was talented. But he had a habit of overestimating his strengths sometimes. He wanted too much, maybe."

"And we don't?" Darcy said.

"Yeah, yeah, I know. I . . . I don't know what I mean about Willy. It's just . . . all . . . sad. All of it. It just would be *him* to get—"

"To get killed," Miranda said bitterly.

"I feel so responsible," Mat said. "When he called to say he was on the way up here, I could've said no. I could've told him we had a full house up here. But I let him have his way."

"Like most of us," Beth said.

Mat nodded. "Yes. I guess nobody ever put the brakes on under him. Maybe he'd be alive if—"

"And maybe another one of us would have been in that barn last night—or somewhere else on the grounds," Ben protested. "Would it make you feel any better if one of the girls were lying dead now?"

For a few moments, no one spoke.

"I think this little wake has had it," Darcy said at last. "I'd just as soon not dwell on any of us lying dead anywhere." She got to her feet and the others began to follow suit.

It was only then that anyone seemed to acknowledge that I was in the room. Beth called out to me, "Alice, you can sleep in the room next to me. Do you know the way?"

They were all moving so slowly, shuffling, half-asleep. I don't think anyone even heard me when I answered, "I'll find it. Thanks."

3

I thought I was dreaming. I heard choking sounds. Mournful sounds. Terrible, heartbroken sighs.

They were all real. I wasn't dreaming.

My room was cold, and almost punitively small in relation to the other bedrooms. Perhaps long ago a child's nurse had used the room, or an au pair.

I knew from the purplish quality of the dark that the sun would be up soon. I got out of bed and walked soundlessly over to the door that connected my room to Beth's. Yes, it was she who was crying. When the weeping went on with no sign of stopping, I decided to go in.

I knocked a few times, not knowing whether she could hear me, and then opened the door. Beth sat up in the four-poster bed. She was red-eyed, and the white comforter was littered with mint-green Kleenex.

"Beth? Beth, is there anything I can do for you?" I approached the bed gingerly, knowing I was meddling. But as soon as I sat next to her, she fell into my arms and wept until the tears were all gone.

"Thanks, Alice. Please forgive me for carrying on like this."

"No need to apologize. You've lost someone close."

"Yes. But it isn't just Will I'm upset about. Just about everything in my life seems to be falling apart at the moment."

I waited, asking nothing, while she blew her nose one final time.

"I told you about the debacle with the Europe thing. Well, I think it did much more damage than we even knew. Mat thought that coming up here was a way to heal us, but I think it's ripping us apart. Maybe for the first time ever, we're taking a look at each other—and not liking what we see."

"Does this have anything to do with Miranda's sniping earlier?" I asked.

"Sure. Even on a good day she's got a pretty sharp tongue. But she's been lashing out, just mad at the world these last few days. I think it's like Roz said: She's scared, too." Beth balled up one of the tissues and sent it flying across the room. "Score another one for Roz," she said, her mouth a little awry.

"Why is everybody so scared? Bad reviews are inevitable. As inevitable as falling out and bickering among friends. You've been together for years. Surely this isn't your first disappointment?"

"No. Well, no *and* yes. We've worked like dogs to make it in the music world. I don't know whether it's true or not that we had to be twice as good as a group of men. But we decided we'd better be. Of course, not everything turned out just the way we wanted it, but we've had great luck—with audiences, with critics, money, the whole thing.

"And we have Mat to thank for everything. He may be a bit of a stick sometimes, but we owe everything to him. In fact, I wonder if it would be harder on him than anyone else if . . . if . . . something happened to us."

"Something like what, Beth?"

She shook her head, as if to clear it of awful thoughts. "I don't know. I guess I'm making things even worse than they are, Alice. It's like I said: Things are just coming unwrapped. And I miss Will. He's not even gone a day, and I miss him already. I never felt lonely when he was around."

New shadows fell across her face. "It's like some kind of morbid preview of what's to come. Do you know what I mean? Have you ever felt you were really down in a hole—maybe the worst place you'd ever been—but you knew the bad stuff wasn't over yet? There was something even worse right around the corner?"

I gave her bleak question, with all its mixed metaphors, some thought. But not much.

"Look, Beth, you should try to get some sleep."

"Can't," she said simply.

"Why don't I look around the kitchen for some tea, something herbal to help you"—I almost said "relax"—"to help you sleep."

She shrugged. I headed back to my room to get a robe.

"Sorry, Alice," I heard come floating toward me. I turned back to her. "Sorry we're ruining your vacation," she said.

I groped around for a minute before locating the kitchen light switch. The lights popped on and I gasped, startled by the sudden movement all around me. I guess I must have been expecting Mrs. Wallace to be standing there with a meat clever.

What I saw was considerably more benign. All around me were plump, tufted, adorable little brown field mice—on top of the cabinets, on the counters, playing games in the toaster.

Where on earth was Lulu, the cat? This was her whole excuse for joining the party. The mice scurried off and I found the kettle and the tea bags.

I located a tray as well, and I was balancing it carefully as I started back up the stairs. I got another scare when I heard someone ask sharply from the gloom of the living room: "Who is that?"

I recognized Miranda Bly's low, whiskey voice.

"It's Alice Nestleton."

"Oh. What's going on?" she asked wearily.

"Nothing really. Beth's having a bad night, and I'm just bringing her some tea."

"Are you now?" Her mocking laughter sounded hollow in the empty room.

"Listen, um ... Alice," she said haltingly, "would you come in here for just a minute?"

I set the tray down in the hallway and joined her.

She didn't switch on the lamp, and didn't have to, because the first light of day had started rolling through the room.

"I really should apologize to you, you know," Miranda said. "I've been filthy to you, and just want you to know I know I have."

"Stressful times," I answered. "It's all right."

"Well, thank you for understanding." She lit a

cigarette and picked up a cut-glass tumbler, containing, I guessed, Scotch. Clearly, she was drunk.

"So, Alice, do tell, what has Beeswax been telling you to enlist your sympathy? Still playing the sensitive wallflower?"

"I'm not sure what she's playing, Miranda. Or even that she's playing at all. But then, I don't know Beth very well. We're just friendly acquaintances. As you said earlier, I'm her cat person."

"Then let me assure you that she most certainly is playing—at something or other." Miranda ran her left hand through her lushly waved hair. I hadn't paid much attention during all the unhappiness of the evening, but she, too, was a beauty, in her way. Her face was pale and moon-shaped and slightly pitted, and she was the only member of the group who was starting to look her age. Hers was the strange, graying beauty of a Lotte Lenya. And her stark black leotard made her appearance all the more arresting.

"Well," I answered carefully, "of course you'd know better than I, but her grief over Will's murder seems completely genuine to me. She's very, very upset."

"When you get to know her better, you'll realize she'd lie about the temperature. She simply doesn't know what the truth is, that girl. And there's no more truth in her grief than there is in her playing."

"But why wouldn't Beth be as sorry about the murder as the rest of you?"

"Because, Alice Armchair, she threatened to kill him herself."

"Excuse me?"

"What's the matter—didn't you hear me? It's true, I tell you. Will had a great sense of play. He played with life. He played with people. And as of late he'd been playing with her."

"Beth was having an affair with him, you mean."

Miranda laughed again, heartlessly. "You might call it that. But from his end of it, they were having something a sight more vulgar than that. I suppose she thought it wasn't high-minded enough, and she wanted something more from him."

"Such as?"

"Oh, for godsakes, how should I know what Beth wants from a man? I just know they'd been having it off ever since he arrived up here. And then the shit hit the fan. I was passing by one of their little trysting places—that shed near the creek—only two days ago. I supposed they'd just done it and were having a row. At any rate, I heard her call him a few names I never expected that little twit to know. They were actually physically fighting in there—throwing things at each other. And when she stormed out, I distinctly heard her say she wanted to kill him."

"I see," I replied after a moment. "Are you sure it wasn't the kind of thing anyone might say in the heat of a terrible argument? What makes you take it so literally in Beth's case?"

"Because . . . when little worms turn, they turn with a vengeance. Second-rate, jealous-hearted little worms in particular."

I sat for just another minute before rising from

my chair. "I think I'd better turn in now, Miranda," I said. "You should sleep, too."

As I suspected, Beth had fallen asleep. She was curled up tightly, as if defending herself from those other blows the world was about to deal her. I saw a ball of shredded tissue in her fist.

And I'd thought I was tired *before*.

Miranda Bly had an iron knot of resentment and contempt inside her. Would she make up a story like the one she'd told me? How was I to know? If there was any truth to it, the police had to be told—*if* there was any truth to it. And how was I to know that?

It would mean shedding my passive observer role, delving, snooping, opening up who knew how many cans of worms. But I *would* know.

And I wondered how Ford would feel about that.

4

I believe it was Saint Augustine who said that all creatures become depressed after making love. But before that bittersweet mood sets in, after the so-called little death, there is first a feeling of complete discombobulation, isn't there? I had recently spent a wonderful, unplanned weekend with someone, and it wasn't until we were parting—reluctantly, regretfully, late Sunday evening—that I recalled how little I actually liked him.

That was the kind of disorientation written on the faces of the temporary residents of the Covington Center for the Arts that morning after Will Gryder's murder. We'd all slept late.

In ones and twos they came down the stairs and groped for coffee from the huge urn Mrs. Wallace had set up in the dining room. Everyone took a turn casting a furtive glance at the uniformed officer ambling around the grounds. Eventually everyone began to talk, but not really to one another. Then the fog began to lift from everyone's mind, but there was still no real eye contact being made. Yet, oddly, the members of the group seemed composed. Each was civil, each had dressed himself or herself carefully enough. It was as though all were fighting to remain in control.

I sat alone in one of the dim little alcoves that seemed to be ubiquitous throughout the enormous house. Well, I wasn't utterly alone: I was having a conversation with Lulu the cat. I had already told her that, quite frankly, she'd better get cracking, or the field mice were going to destroy her reputation, and forever besmirch the reputation of Scottish Folds everywhere. Lulu seemed not at all concerned about that, curled up and alternately snoozing and purring in my lap.

I could hear disjointed snatches of conversation from the nearby dining room. There was a bit of gallows humor: some speculation about what would happen to Will's splendid six-room, rent-controlled apartment between Columbus and Central Park West. Then I heard Ben Polikoff's grave voice say that if some thief had murdered Will for the cash in his pockets, then everyone had better be doubly careful because, after all, there were literally hundreds of thousands of dollars worth of musical instruments in the house—Roz's violin being particularly valuable.

When I went in to join them, I was startled by their weird mixture of lethargy and tension. Everyone managed a friendly greeting for me. Except Miranda, whose stuporous silence seemed more the telltale sign of a hangover than of any rancor she may have been feeling toward me. I still had Lulu in my arms. It gave me something to hold on to.

It had been drizzling all morning, but the rain wasn't cold. Then, around eleven, the sun came out and the air grew unexpectedly sweet and warm. The ground outside was thawing into muddy slush as water from the leaves of the mighty chestnut dripped down.

Mrs. Wallace kept gamely trying to interest us in brunch. What was our pleasure? Fresh muffins? eggs? pasta? quiche? But there were no takers. Grumbling, she folded her apron and went about her chores outside.

Darcy, in a close-fitting T-shirt and black jeans which showed off her marvelous little figure, engaged me in a brief conversation about Al Pacino, her favorite actor, and about the theater in general and my own career. But our chat quickly petered out. I suppose she was just trying to make me feel a little more at ease.

A few minutes later Ben rose from his place energetically, announcing that he was going to take Roz into Northampton. A nice lunch out and a little shopping would do her a world of good, he insisted, looking down at her bent figure. Maybe they could even take in a movie. And anyone who felt like coming along was welcome, he said.

Just about ready to start climbing the walls, I jumped at the chance to tag along with them. I was the only one to do so. The others murmured their excuses, or said nothing, and one by one began drifting out of the room. I brushed my teeth, changed quickly into a skirt and blouse, and was ready in less than ten minutes.

I followed Roz and Ben as they walked out of the house arm-in-arm. Her wild red hair seemed to give off sparks in the afternoon light. Was she really grasping Ben's arm for dear life—or was it he who was gripping her so tightly? I couldn't tell.

The seat covers of the chocolate-brown Mercedes were opulent leather. I slid comfortably into the back. Roz, seated in front of me, seemed to be fending off her private gloom; her face kept twisting and untwisting, as if she were making the effort to think only of better times.

As we were pulling away, Ben suddenly stopped and cut the motor, cocking his ear. I knew what he was listening to. Miranda's cello was floating through the lovely, mournful "Swan" andantino from *The Carnival of Animals*, by Saint-Saëns. The three of us sat listening until the piece was finished.

It was Roz who broke the silence. She shook her head a little before speaking. "Heavenly, wasn't it?" she said. "Almost as if she was capable of some . . . genuine . . . individual . . . tenderness."

Ben expertly wheeled the Mercedes up the winding gravel path and out onto the main road. "Ever been up in these parts before, Alice?" He was looking at me in the rearview mirror.

Ben Polikoff looked like such a vital man— extremely healthy, competent, self-possessed, sophisticated. It didn't seem to square with his almost childish dependence on and constant attention to his wife, as though she were an invalid, or as though her slightest unhappiness unbalanced him.

"Yes, I've spent some time in Northampton," I answered. "I once taught a workshop at Smith."

"Is that so? But you didn't go to Smith?" he asked, a gentle smile on his face.

"Now, Ben, do I look like a Smith girl to you?"

"Yes," he said immediately. "In fact you do—tall and blond and beautiful."

It was one of the rawest compliments I have ever received, but I really didn't take it as one.

"You know, there was a rude little ditty in my day, Alice. As a sort of Smith alumna, I hope you won't be offended."

"I'm sure I won't."

"The fellows used to say, when it came to dating, 'Smith to bed, Mt. Holyoke to wed.' "

The "fellows," I assumed, were pathetic Harvard frat boys who got tight on beer and their own fantasies. I laughed politely, catching Ben's eye in the mirror.

I leaned back into the leather seat. What a difference there was between this humming, responsive vehicle and the one I'd rented for the drive up here! I felt as if I could ride five hundred miles in this one without experiencing a jot of fatigue.

"Maybe I should just keep going till we reach Tanglewood," Ben quipped. "Maybe Seiji is doing something interesting this afternoon." It was a feeble joke. The Tanglewood music festival was a summer affair. But it must have been some kind of private joke between them, for Roz extended one hand and very slowly and affectionately began to massage her husband's neck.

"Do you get to Tanglewood often, Alice?" he asked.

"Oh, Ben," Roz interjected a little chastisingly, a little patronizingly, too, "she's an *actress*." As though somehow actors were forestalled from attending such events. As though we, as a class, were culturally retarded, if forgivably so.

I would have responded testily, but I realized that Roz wasn't entirely responsible for what she was saying. The grief lines still creased her forehead.

We drove on in contented silence for a while.

"I hope you'll join us for lunch," Ben said, speaking, obviously, to me. "There's a fine new Italian place on Main Street."

"Sounds terrific," I said, secretly checking for Roz's reaction. I could see none.

Brilliant sunlight was pouring into the car now. It felt warm and renewing on my neck and shoulders. I closed my eyes, truly luxuriating in the ride. I felt that I could quite easily fall . . . fast asleep . . . lulled by the happy purr . . . of the engine.

Then Roz screamed.

"Ben!" she shrieked. "A dog, Ben! Watch—"

I heard the awful screech of brakes. Saw a blur of brown fur before my body twisted and the force of the skid sent me hurtling forward. Then the whole world was brown.

5

It was quiet. So quiet I knew I couldn't be dead.

I pushed myself up and back onto the seat. For a minute I just sat there staring foolishly out of the window. The car had executed a wild turn: Half on the road and half off, the front end was now facing in the direction from which we had come.

I feel fine, I told myself. Just fine. And my head is so ... so light! I sat waiting happily for the drive to recommence.

A strangling noise from the front seat jolted me back to reality. Roz was thrashing about, trying to get out of her seatbelt. Ben wasn't moving at all. His belt had prevented him from smacking into the window, but he seemed to have hit the top of the wheel, and now he was collapsed over it. Roz's struggle had become crazed by now.

I opened the back door and climbed out. My legs buckled for just a moment, then they became strong again. I tried Roz's door. It was still locked from the inside. I banged on her window. She looked at me wild-eyed. I gestured that she should open the door from the inside. But she didn't understand. I got back into the backseat, reached over and opened the latch in front. Then

I slipped out again and pulled her door open. Her thin frame seemed to be wracked with spasms.

"Be still, Roz—*be still!*"

My plea brought her to her senses. She was breathing heavily, gagging, but at last she calmed. I undid the seat belt quickly and helped her out, gingerly leaning her against the side of the car.

Then I hurried to the other side to see about Ben. He was dazed, bleeding rather badly from the forehead, but conscious. "I'm all right," he croaked. "I'm . . ."

"Stay where you are, Ben," I warned, unbuckling his seat belt. A ridiculous instruction—where was he going to go? "Just stay there. I'll get help."

I ran up the other side of the road, looking for a car to flag down. Two went by without stopping. But then, a minute later, a bread truck braked and the driver climbed out, stared into the Mercedes, and told me he'd call the police from the gas station two miles down the road.

There were two local police cars and an ambulance. The medics began very carefully to extricate Ben from the car, while Roz and I wearily answered the officers' questions. These men were a lot less polished, more New England folksy than the state police who were investigating Will Gryder's murder.

When the questioning was finished, Roz turned to me in desperation. "Oh, God! That dog! What happened to that poor dog? It's probably lying somewhere, suffering. We have to find it, Alice. Please."

Yes, she was right of course. I couldn't let the

poor thing suffer. I had to find it. So, while Ben was being eased into the ambulance, I started my search—up and down the shoulders of both sides of the road. I could find nothing, though. No dog, living, dying, or dead.

Then, in growing fear, I began to search for bloodstains. But there weren't any of those, either. Was it possible the dog had escaped unhurt? I hoped that was the case.

I looked a while longer and then gave up and started back toward the car. I could see the tracks my boots had made in the slush.

That's right! I could *see* the tracks my boots had made. Why hadn't I thought of that before? There was a dog in the road and it was crossing in front of the car when Roz cried out—so where were its tracks? It must have left prints in the muddy ground, just as I had. Why couldn't I find them anywhere?

I looked up to see the police officers waving me back to the Mercedes. I signaled that I'd be just a few minutes longer.

I crisscrossed the road again. There were tire tracks in the sludge, and footprints, but no paw prints. None at all. What I did notice were curious, elongated marks. It looked very much as if someone had dragged a sled across the mud.

I couldn't understand it. We had all seen the dog flash across the road—or so we thought. But of *course* it was a dog. It may have all been a blur, but it *had* been there. It had been what made Ben swerve off the road.

Still confused, I walked back to the others. Roz went with Ben in the ambulance. One of the officers helped me into his patrol car and drove me back to the Center.

They were all there waiting for me.

Obviously on Roz's instructions, the police had phoned the house to tell everyone there about the accident. Beth and Darcy and Mathew and the cook—yes, and even Miranda—were all so solicitous of my welfare. For which I was grateful, because five minutes after I entered the house the full impact of what had happened hit me. I was weak, trembling. Mrs. Wallace prepared a giant cup of cocoa for me. Darcy wrapped a blanket around my shoulders. Miranda took off my boots. And Beth, while chafing my hands, barked out other instructions related to my comfort to Mat Hazan, who kept muttering as he obeyed them, "This place is nothing but a chamber of horrors."

A while later, Roz phoned from the hospital. Darcy took the call and relayed the news to us: Both Polikoffs were okay. Ben had to have a few stitches for the head wound, but there had been little damage other than that. They were going to keep him in hospital for a day or two, and Roz would remain with him. But everything was going to be fine.

Soon Beth was taking me by the arm and leading me up the long staircase. "Time you had a nap, Alice. We'll put you in Roz and Ben's room. It's more comfortable there."

We went up together, slowly, and Beth eased me down onto the old four-poster. "No need to undress," she said, seemingly from a dozen miles away. "Just lie back and I'll cover you with this quilt."

The last thing I remembered was a feeling of shame—shame that I'd been so wiped out by a minor traffic accident, while the sight of Will

Gryder's gruesome corpse, grotesquely impaled by the weapon buried in his chest, had not noticeably fazed me. There was something very strange about that.

I awoke to find the last light of afternoon painting the big windows in the Polikoffs' room. I must not have had any bad dreams, because I felt completely rested, at peace. Staring at me from the armchair cushion were the bright round eyes of Lulu.

"Well, hi, kiddo!" I called out. "You're supposed to be downstairs, you know. That's where the mice are." The cat blinked a few times, then she hopped off the chair and trotted over to the bed. She situated herself in the crook of my arm and sniffed me amiably.

My throat was dry, but I was too comfortable to get up for water. The door was cracked open and I could hear voices downstairs. The scent of roasting meat and rosemary soon reached me. How pleasant it all seemed—I was in a lovely old house in New England on a beautiful autumn evening. Downstairs was a group of lively, talented people waiting for me to join them. There was a sensational meal in the oven and probably a great bottle of wine already opened and waiting.

Nice daydream. Except that every element of it was just a little off. I had been thrown into contact with a group of people who were certainly bright enough, but I wasn't sure they cared very much for me—and maybe not even for one another. There had been a terrible murder here. And today I'd almost been killed.

The motor accident came back to me then in

detail. We had been very lucky. It might have been much worse if the car had not skidded in a circle and ended up back on the road. The Mercedes might have gone off the shoulder completely, into an embankment; it might have flipped over. Or suppose there'd been another car on the road! Lucky indeed. We might all have been killed.

And what about the dog who'd caused the accident? I couldn't stop thinking about it. I hadn't been able to find any trace of it. Why not? Trying not to disturb Lulu too much, I propped myself up against the bed pillows. I was trying to remember that moment just before the crash. Roz had screamed out a warning. *"A dog, Ben!"* she had said. Then I saw that brown blur. I hadn't questioned that it was a dog. But where were its tracks on the muddy road?

The cat rose up and stretched expansively. "Well, kiddo?" I flicked at her ears. "Answer me that. What happened to his tracks? Was he hurt or not? Was he there or not?" Lulu climbed off the quilt and thumped out of the room. I chuckled to myself. "What a useless creature," I said aloud. "No mice, no answers."

I reclined again and stared out of the window. Almost full night now. The trees were beginning to appear threatening.

I finally got myself out of bed and walked over to the old dresser, regarding myself in the mirror. I was a mess. After washing up in Roz and Ben's little bathroom, I borrowed a barrette for my hair and then used a cotton ball to apply what I took to be Roz's facial toner. I looked at the label on it and saw that it had come from Kiehl's, a venerable Lower East Side institution that custom-makes cosmetics and perfumes for its customers.

The scent of the cologne in the little bottle I'd opened was transporting. I stood there sniffing it, thinking. I had been foolish to put those questions to little Lulu. But the really important question, I hadn't even asked: Why was I obsessed with the brown dog?

I guess I already knew why, though. Knew it kind of fearfully. It was because the accident might not have been an accident at all. It might have been all too deliberate. Someone, perhaps the same person who had murdered Will Gryder, might have wanted to kill me. Or either of the Polikoffs. Or all three of us. I put the cologne away.

Clues? Motives? Possible scenarios? I had none to back up my belief, but the belief was there just the same. That's just how I felt. It was an informed guess, based no doubt on the timing of things—the coincidence of both events. Gryder is murdered about eight o'clock in the evening by person or persons unknown. Sixteen hours later three suspects in the killing—and I knew that Ford Donaldson more or less had to consider us all suspects—are almost killed in an accident.

I'd done as much repair work on my appearance as I could, but I went on regarding my face in the mirror.

Mirror mirror on the wall,
Why get involved in this case at all?

My image grimaced, then said to me: "And if you *wanted* to get involved in this case . . . where would you start? You know nothing except what Lieutenant Donaldson told you."

"Not true," I told her, smiling. I knew something that Donaldson himself didn't know. I knew that Beth and Will had made love in a shed on the premises, and then fought violently. Miranda had told me so. And now I believed her. And I knew that the first thing I should do was take a look at the shed. All this because of a dog who was supposed to be there but wasn't—not even his paw prints.

I was overwhelmingly thirsty now. I went down to get a drink and join that glowing house party of the imagination.

6

Around six-thirty the following morning I tip-toed slowly down the stairs, being careful not to wake the others. I wanted to get out of the house without anyone noticing. I didn't quite know why I was being so secretive—there was really nothing to hide.

At any rate, all that stealth turned out to be futile, for the kitchen was ablaze with light and Mrs. Wallace was busily at her morning's work. I was suddenly aware of those universal good-food smells.

"Aren't you the little early bird this morning?" she said from the stove, not even turning to look at me.

I went in to the kitchen and headed directly for the door that opened onto a small storeroom, which in turn led outside. This rear entrance to the house was closer to the creek than the front door was.

"Good morning, Mrs. Wallace," I said, trying to sound casual. "I thought I'd take a nice long walk this morning because it's so . . . so lovely."

She cast a quick glance out of the kitchen window at the thick gray sky.

"The *grounds* are so lovely, I mean. And I

haven't had much of a chance to see the property."

"Yes," she said dully. "Then you'll want to take some nourishment first, I'm sure." With one foot she quickly pulled out a kitchen chair and nodded to me that it was my place at the table.

Obeying, I sat down, and continued to trip over my own words. "Thanks . . . and did I thank you enough for that wonderful meal last night? I don't think I've ever had veal so fragrant and moist. And those potatoes!"

"Anna," she grunted.

"Oh, yes. Potatoes Anna. Superb."

Mrs. Wallace then dropped a plate in front of me. "And what," she said, a sardonic little smile on her face, "did you think of the dessert?"

I looked down at the neatly cut wedge of an exquisitely turned-out omelet. "The dessert? Superb, also." And it *had* been—a rich, undecorated slice of cake in a little pool of perfect *crème anglaise*.

She placed her own plate on the table then. Her half of the omelet was just as beautiful, cooked precisely the way I like it, folded over but still thin and burnished on the top. She set about removing the plastic wrap from three small bowls on the table. One contained red caviar, one black—leftovers from last Sunday's brunch—and the last held what I took to be sour cream. No, it wasn't sour cream, Mrs. Wallace corrected me. It was *fromage frais*, which she'd served with berries a few nights ago. Hadn't I ever heard of its American equivalent, "creole cream cheese"? I had to confess my ignorance.

Last, she brought a plate of piping hot English muffins, fresh from the blackened griddle on which she'd made them, and a battered old percolator full of coffee that was still bubbling up against the glass nipple in the lid.

I hadn't been the least bit hungry ten minutes ago, but I tucked into the food lustily. "How does a person get to be such a wonderful cook?" I asked, genuinely interested.

She sipped her coffee complacently. "Ever hear of Lydie Marshall?" she asked.

"No, I don't believe so."

"What about Simone Beck?"

The name sounded vaguely familiar, but I didn't know why. I shook my head in answer.

"But surely you've heard of James Beard, Julia Child."

"Yes, of course," I said. "Did you study with them all?"

"I surely did, my girl. I surely did. Now, wouldn't you think in most places that would earn a person some kind of respect . . . some kind of . . . ?" Her voice trailed off in irritation.

Mrs. Wallace barely touched her food. Instead, she watched closely as I consumed mine. "I have plenty more muffins where those came from," she told me when I'd cleaned my plate. "What about another one with some of my preserves? I can see you're not one of those weak women that never eat a good meal, always watching their so-called figures."

I managed to prevent her from feeding me more than one additional muffin, and while she was at the sink, I seized the opportunity to push away from the table and throw on the old sheepskin coat.

"Well, thank you for breakfast," I said quickly. "I think I'll go on that walk now."

"Hmm," she mumbled. "You'll probably freeze."

It *was* damned cold! So much for the Indian Summer yesterday had promised. I strode away from the house and then stopped twenty feet away to get my bearings.

In the distance I could see the big barn—Will Gryder's studio. I found the path I had taken that night with Beth, the night we'd found his body. Then I took the connecting path, which ran past the back of the studio and meandered into a wooded plot. Through the trees I could make out two small structures. These, I assumed, were the sheds I'd heard mentioned, and the creek must be just beyond. I picked up my pace, eager to leave the forbidding barn behind.

Just as I reached the woods I heard, once again, a disembodied cello. I was not only enchanted by the beautiful sounds it was making, I was also confused—it couldn't be Miranda again, not at this hour. It was much too early. I knew the piece well: Bach's C Major Suite for Unaccompanied Cello. I had owned Casals' recording of it for years, but then the record was lost in one of my many moves. It could have been a record I was hearing now. But where was it coming from?

The studio? Was it possible the music was coming from Will's studio? Yes! I stood listening for another minute. How macabre. I turned back and made for the barn. But I hesitated at the door, frightened to go in. Then, as suddenly as the music had begun, it stopped. I waited a few seconds longer, then opened the door and peered in. The studio was deserted. I stepped back outside and closed the door, thinking that the music would start again any minute. But it never came. There was nothing but country morning silence. Had the traffic accident shaken something loose in my brain? Would I keep hearing music wherever I went?

I made my way through the woods, the frozen twigs snapping beneath my boots. I found the shed easily—two sheds, actually, within a few feet of each other—about fifty feet from a stream. It must have been a respectable stream once; the sides were steep enough, but now the near-frozen flow was minimal, pretty pathetic. Logs and chunks of metal stuck out of the creek bed, as if it had become a local dumping place.

The sheds were like old-fashioned beach cabanas, made of wood and metal. A sliding door was at the front of each. They were only about ten feet deep but they were quite long, almost the size of Quonset huts.

I slid open the door of the shed closest to the creek. It was musty and frigid inside. A central aisle, very narrow, led from one end of the structure to the other, and on either side of the aisle were trunks and cartons—a vast array of assorted junk, including old clothes tied into uneven bales.

All of it had been left behind, intentionally or unintentionally, by the artists who'd resided at the colony over the years.

At the very end of the aisle, I found a space where someone obviously had pushed some cartons away and heaved others onto a neighboring pile. This afforded only a small space, but there were two blankets on the floor, an old pillow tied at the ends, and two empty brandy bottles.

Was this the place where, according to Miranda, Beth and Will had made love and then fought? It certainly could be. The bedding and the bottles seemed to hint at some kind of tryst.

I had to wonder why they would meet here in this cramped, dirty, cold place. Why hadn't they gone to any of the half-dozen motels in the Northampton area? Or even better, to one of the perfectly comfortable cabins right here on the grounds, where they could build a cozy fire in the wood-burning stove?

I stared down at the blankets. Maybe, I thought, Will Gryder had been one of those men who love illicit sex . . . who get turned on by stolen sex accomplished at the wrong time in the wrong place for the wrong reason . . . sex as a kind of adventuring theft. There were men like that. Even my friend Tony Basillio would, on occasion, rather make love in a phone booth on the Jersey Turnpike that in a suite at the Plaza. It was some kind of twisted behavior that many men exhibit. And many women accept it, even if they find it absurd.

Absurd? My response to this trysting place—I had looked away—suddenly made me feel very uncomfortable. Was I becoming a total prude in my middle age? My goodness! There was a time in my life when I had made love in much more illicit places and thought it perfectly natural. And rather exciting. And I had been the one who had initiated it. I looked down again.

There was something very sad about those soiled old blankets. They didn't say that Beth had killed Gryder, but they did point to her as a suspect. And that wasn't the only sad thing

about this place. There was just something so . . .
seedy about it.

I closed up the first shed and went on to the
other one. The door of that one was harder to
open. Something seemed to have caught on one
of the sliding hinges. But finally it yielded and I
walked inside. Like the other hut, this one was
filled with the detritus of the decades—things
tossed, wrapped, bundled. I wondered if Will
and Beth had made love in this shed as well. I
walked to the center aisle, ready to start my in-
spection. But I had to stop. It was too dark to see
much of anything. There was an overhead bulb
as in the other shed, but there was no wall
switch for this fixture. I flailed around, searching
for a pull of some sort, and when I found none,
I stood on tiptoes and managed to reach the
bulb and turn it gently. The light was weak, but
it illuminated the room just fine. I turned down
the aisle.

Suddenly I froze in absolute horror. I threw
my hands up in front of my face, between me
and the hideous face that loomed in front of me.

Then my shock dissolved into embarrassed
laughter. I was staring into the eyes of a camel.
A big, brown, goofy-faced camel, on a rocker!
An enormous stuffed animal, the kind some
girls cherish from cradle to college dorm. It was
perched on top of a dusty carton.

I reached up and squeezed its dark brown
nose.

I was once going to buy Basillio just such a
toy; that was right after he'd broken up with his
wife. He was so terribly lonely, and I had a few
dollars in radio commercial residuals coming to
me. So I went into FAO Schwarz and found this

wonderful rocking camel. I fell absolutely in love with the thing. The only problem was the price tag—$297. I didn't buy it.

Well, Basillio didn't need this kind of company any more, thankfully. I reached up to give the dear old thing one last pat. And as I did so, my hand brushed against its underside, which was wet and gritty.

I stepped up to take a closer look. Not only was the camel's belly wet, the rocker on which he stood was streaked with mud, as if it had been dragged through slush of some kind.

I went cold all over. I was remembering the marks I had found yesterday when looking for the injured dog. *Like a sled*, I had thought then, like a sled pulled across the muddy road.

So *this* was the mysterious brown dog! This silly toy camel was what had caused the accident. Someone had pulled it across the path in front of us, to make us crash. But who? And which one of us did that someone want dead?

The camel was moving almost imperceptibly, peacefully rocking. But my fear was increasing with its every movement.

Enough cute stuff, I decided right then. Enough exploring and dabbling. This was serious, and I was getting mad. It didn't matter whether he thought he was Clint Eastwood or Joel McCrea—I needed to speak to Ford Donaldson.

7

"You're a very hard man to reach, Lieutenant Donaldson."

"Is that so?" Donaldson turned his impassive face to me. "Well, I'm sorry if I kept you waiting, but we're pretty busy these days—whether you and your friends believe it or not."

"Please don't misunderstand. I—" I started to explain. I wanted to assure him I realized he was working hard to solve the Gryder killing. But he didn't let me finish.

"This town isn't quite as sleepy as some folks might think," he said sarcastically.

"No," I said carefully. "And obviously neither are you, Lieutenant."

My rejoinder startled him into a minute's silence. Long enough for me to go on to make my point.

"As I was going to say, there are a few things I think you'll want to know. I thought it was best to tell you in private, but it's been a little difficult reaching you."

A little difficult, to say the least. I'd had to go through all kinds of channels before this audience was granted. I had to speak to the officer on duty on the premises at the house, who'd given me a phone number to call. Then there

was a secretary to get by. And another policeman, who agreed to pass on the message to
Donaldson only after he'd phoned the house to
speak to the one on-duty there. Finally I'd been
instructed to wait for a call from the man himself. When it finally came, I'd had to convince
Lt. Donaldson that I knew something important
enough to make it worth his while to see me
alone. It was all so Byzantine—needlessly so, I
was betting.

By the time Ford's newly washed, gas-
efficient, no-nonsense car stopped on the road
just off the Covington Center property, the heat
seemed to have been turned up a notch under
whatever the personal crisis was that made him
so touchy and sour.

His mood had not affected him sartorially,
though: He was as fastidiously put together as
that first night we met. This time he was a sym-
phony of brown—shoes, trousers, shirt, and all
in subtly differing shades. As I settled myself on
the passenger side in front, I noticed a beautiful
Stetson on the back seat.

The car moved off noiselessly.

"Well," he said, "alone at last."

"Yes," I said. "Thank you for taking the time."

"There isn't that much of it, I'm afraid. By the
way, from what I hear, you were lucky to walk
away from that thing yesterday. Accident like
that—could've been much worse. I hear your
friends are going to walk away from it, too."

"The Polikoffs are not my *friends*," I said testily, knowing how that sounded but unable to
stop myself. "I'm sure you had other things on
your mind, Lieutenant, when you spoke to us

after the killing. But I thought I explained my position in the house then."

He did not respond. I saw him look up at the road sign that announced ENTERING HARRODS-VILLE, and then he made a swift turn. A half-consumed pack of LifeSavers rolled gently across the dashboard toward the wheel.

"I guess I could use a cup of coffee," he said then. "You can tell me in the diner just as well as here. This time of day Miss Edna's is just as . . . private . . . as anywhere else."

I hoped this signaled a break in the man's stoic frontiersman bit. He helped himself to one of the candies, and I wondered vaguely if sugar was playing some part in his mood shift.

Miss Edna's Diner was truly a piece of living nostalgia—soda fountain and worn leather booths and a lone waitress in orthopedic shoes. I wondered if any film companies had discovered it. It would make a wonderful location for a period movie.

Donaldson took his time getting around to asking for my information. What with his amiable chitchat with the short-order cook and his minute scrutiny of the pie case before he made his selection, I got the message: I couldn't possibly know anything crucial to *his* investigation.

But finally he was ready to listen. First I improvised thumbnail sketches of the personalities of Miranda and Beth—to the extent that I could do so with any authority. I went on to tell him, as succinctly as possible, about Miranda's revelation to me: that Beth and Will were lovers, and had fought violently not long before the murder. Then about their dusty trysting place in the shed, which seemed only to lend more credence to Miranda's story.

"Well," he said when I'd concluded the recitation, "that certainly is interesting."

It was hard to know what to say. My mocking little laugh came out in a kind of snort. "Right. I agree it is 'interesting.' " I waited while he drank more coffee. And waited.

"You know," he said at last, "two things occur to me. First of all, it looked to me like the members of that musical group are none too fond of each other. Something's seriously . . . amiss with those friends of yours."

I didn't take the bait this time, so he continued. "And then, number two, I have to figure a story like that is full of . . . a lot of . . ."

"A lot of *what*, Lieutenant?"

"A lot of wild exaggeration, Miss Nestleton."

My heartbeat picked up by a few blips. Ford Donaldson was one of the most infuriating people I'd ever encountered.

"What are you saying, Lieutenant Donaldson? That I've gotten hold of a few seamy rumors and I'm carried away with them? That *I'm* guilty of wild exaggeration?"

I had delivered the last line to the back of his neck, because he was signaling the waitress for a refill. I suddenly understood how satisfying it must be for one man to tap another on the shoulder and then knock him to the ground.

"Oh, no," he said when he'd turned back to me. "Not necessarily you. The exaggeration could be all Miss Bly's."

"And what would the exaggeration be: that Beth and Will might have slept together, but their fight wasn't serious at all?"

"Maybe. Maybe something like that."

"But I have no reason to distrust Miranda's story. If I confirmed one part of it, why shouldn't I also believe the other part?"

"But you didn't confirm anything," he said simply. "Not only are you having a problem going from Point A to Point B here, you haven't even got a Point A."

"What do you mean?"

"Look," he said, not unkindly, "you have no way of proving those blankets you saw in the shed were used by Beth and Gryder—or any other two people, for that matter."

"But the story fits!" I insisted.

"Let me explain something to you, Alice. You don't mind if I call you Alice, do you?"

I shrugged. "Anything. Just go on—please."

"You don't know this area very well, Alice. Matter of fact, you don't know it at all."

"No, I don't."

"If you did, you'd know that the local kids like nothing better than violating the 'No Trespassing' signs around that property. They go onto the grounds. They use the creek as a toilet and the unlocked cabins as motels. They steal tools. They write on the side of the house. They make a general nuisance of themselves, 'cause they've got nothing better to do. They're out of school or out of work or they're just plain stupid. Are you starting to get the picture, Alice?"

"You mean, the local people have never liked the Center and all it represents. That they resent the city people coming into their community with their pretensions . . . and their cars . . . and their 'art.' "

"No, Alice," he said wearily. "I don't mean

that at all. I said *some* kids get up to all kinds of nonsense. Dumb punks. Not the people in 'the community,' as you call it. Most people appreciate what the Covington School has done for the town.

"Why do you keep calling it a school?"

"Because that's how it started out, in the Twenties. A local woman who'd been a dancer in Boston came back here and started a school for the children—the children of *this community*—to teach them dancing and painting and every art you can think of. At one time we had artists from all over the world up here teaching us hicks about the finer things.

"The School has been a part of life in these parts for some seventy years. Ask the grocer if he doesn't want their business. Ask Paul Fiske in the liquor store. You think the school doesn't pay property taxes like anybody else? Water bills? People who've stayed there tend to come back up here to vacation. They rent cars, they stay in the bed-and-breakfast places. They buy books in the bookstore. They—"

"All right, Lieutenant Donaldson! I think I'm beginning to see."

"Hope so."

He had made some points I couldn't brush off. And not merely the socioeconomic lecture he'd just delivered. Yes, I supposed it was possible that it could have been local teenagers who'd made love in the shed. Except for the empty brandy bottles. How likely was it that out-of-work or minimum-wage kids would take Martell's cognac along on a joyride, like a six-pack of Budweiser?

At any rate, I was still convinced that Miranda's story was true. And that the relationship between Beth and Will might have played an important role in the murder.

"Lieutenant Donaldson," I said, "I have to admit everything you've said is also 'interesting.' But I have something else to tell you." I was ready to drop the bombshell now.

"Something else?" he said distractedly, counting out change for the waitress's tip. "What's that, Alice?"

I said somberly, "That accident yesterday was no accident. Someone was trying to kill us—or me—or Roz—or whomever."

That shook him.

I moved in quickly and told him all about my search for the injured dog; about the strange sled-like marks I'd found in the road; and then about the big toy in the shed with the mud on its rocker.

He said not a word to interrupt me. And when I'd finished he burst into laughter.

I sat there, furious all over again, waiting for his merriment to subside.

It did stop, after a few more choking guffaws. And finally his face settled into its old unreadability.

"All done, Ford?"

"Yep. Yeah, Alice, I am." He checked his watch, then asked me very politely, "Need a little more coffee?"

"No, I do not!"

Donaldson leaned forward, toward me, and took on a toneless, very professional air. He then began to fire a series of questions at me.

"Was the car trip into town planned for days in advance?"

"No," I answered, "of course not—that is, I don't see how it could've been. Ben just decided on the spur of the moment and I decided to join them. It was so gloomy in the house. . . ."

"How could an elaborate plan like that have been set into motion on the spur of the moment? It would have required a conspirator somewhere on the road—right?—someone waiting with your stuffed camel and a car phone.

"Somebody would have had to call him from the house, the moment the three of you left, and then he would have had to hide the car somewhere, station himself at a strategic place on the road, wait to catch sight of the Mercedes, and then at the last minute run across the road—or better yet, slide the toy across the road at just the right moment."

He paused briefly, waiting for my response. I had none. He was right: The conspiracy would have had to be almost absurdly elaborate.

"The guy in the car gets a call on his fancy phone saying you three are underway. Okay— how does he know which way the car is going to turn once it leaves the property? You can't even see the road from the house. You can make a left turn or a right turn. There are at least two ways to get into Northampton from Covington—one leads right into the highway, the other takes longer but is more scenic. And what if Polikoff had decided to take the back road, behind the school and through Chelton-ham?"

Again, I had no answer.

"Sounds like the man and his camel would be left high and dry, doesn't it, Alice?"

We were mostly silent on the drive back.

Donaldson pulled up close to the gate and waited for me to leave the car. I had blown it with Good Soldier Ford. He obviously didn't think much of me or my theories. I was terribly embarrassed at not having worked things out more convincingly, and my feelings were hurt, too. But I knew I'd get over all that. Logic might be on his side right now, but it was me someone had tried to kill, not him.

I didn't get out of the car just yet. Seeing me linger, he waited in silence.

"One other thing," I said quietly, not knowing how he'd take what I was about to say. "In spite of today, I . . . I do have some experience . . . as a criminal investigator. Professionally, I mean."

He stared at me in puzzlement.

Should I tell him about the cases I'd solved? Should I list my credentials, say that I had once been a paid consultant to an elite arm of the New York City Police Department? No. I decided not to try to prove to him that I was no fool in these matters.

Instead I simply said, "I would like to offer you whatever help I can in what has been happening here."

"Sure," he said, "we'd really appreciate it."

His tone was so patronizing that I think it embarrassed even him. I wouldn't have been surprised to receive a pat on the head. And to make sure I wouldn't get one, I quickly got out of the car.

I stood shivering on the cold path, watching him drive away. Dispirited as I was, I knew I had to organize my thoughts carefully and make a thoughtful move. I knew I had to go back to the beginning, so to speak. I had to look behind the stated reason for the Riverside Quartet's decision to shut themselves away up here—and find the real one. That inquiry was going to begin with the man who made *all* the decisions for the quartet: Mathew Hazan.

I was just about to turn into the gate when I heard the sound of a motor. Coming back up the drive was the clean, state-issued vehicle I'd come to know so well. Ford Donaldson had forgotten something, perhaps. Or maybe he was in the mood to laugh at me some more.

He motioned me over to his rolled-down window.

"Look, er ... Alice ... I don't like to think you're going away mad. I just wanted to apologize ... if I offended you. And to say that I really would appreciate your help. Look, here's a number where you can always reach me if you learn something else." He pushed a white business card into my hand. I continued to stare daggers into his heart. "Seriously," he said, "I want your help. Understand?"

"Oh, I think I do, Ford," I said, my face a mask. "You need a punch line to the story when you tell it to the boys in the locker room. And don't think they won't appreciate it." The man was cruel. I backed away swiftly and started in through the gate.

"Just a minute!" he exploded.

I froze where I stood.

"Please, just listen for a minute! Let me tell

you something about this case for a change. Okay?"

I turned and went back.

"Everything about this murder points to some juiced-up local bad boy who went into this thing just looking to rip off some rich people and ended up way over his head. He probably thought that barn was empty—who knows? Gryder may have fallen asleep in that chair. He wakes up to find someone robbing the place, and the kid panics and kills him. That's a sensible approach to the case, and so it's the one we've got to pursue. Except there's a hitch with that theory—a great big one. And I wouldn't be telling you about it if I didn't think you had a brain." He paused for a minute. "Or if I thought you'd killed Mr. Gryder."

I nodded my understanding.

"The hitch is that someone in the main house took Gryder's room apart the night he was killed. We know what time he was murdered, but not what time the room was tossed. And if the search happened before the murder ... You're following me here, Alice, right?"

Indeed I was. It sounded as though someone in the house might have been desperately looking for something in Will's room. And when they didn't find it, they went to his studio. However the scenario had unfolded there, that person probably ended up killing him.

I looked deeply into Ford Donaldson's strong face, realizing that he was no longer mocking or patronizing me. Not that I understood the man—far from it. Maybe he was a genuine New England eccentric, maybe he was a tortured soul, or maybe he just had a mean streak. But he would never have imparted information like this to me if he didn't take me seriously.

I stepped away from the car. "Thank you, Lieutenant," I said.

"See you around, Alice."

8

It was getting harder and harder to maintain the fantasy that we were all part of a merry house party. The remaining residents—Mat and Beth and Darcy and Miranda—talked to one another, ate together, listened to music, and sat together by the fire with their brandies. But each seemed to have some private grief or depression gnawing at him or her. Each would briefly emerge from a funk, be communal with the others, and then drop back into silence.

Only one of our number seemed to have no worries: Lulu. She had spent the bulk of the evening snoring peacefully in my lap, having forgiven me completely for my attack on her mousing proficiency. In fact, I guess I had libeled Scottish Folds everywhere. Meanwhile, the field mice were expanding geometrically in the main house. Becoming bolder every day, they had now established residence in the library.

I felt a little weighted down from Mrs. Wallace's all-out *bouffe*—course after course after course of it. But the gloomier we were, the more she fed us. The centerpiece of tonight's meal had been a glorious crown roast of pork with prunes, and I had eaten like a fool.

Mathew Hazan was doing his part as peacemaker/master of ceremonies/hand-holder/ what have you. Early in the day he had been sequestered behind closed doors with Darcy as she rehearsed a difficult Smetana piece she was to perform as guest soloist on an upcoming recording.

Later in the afternoon I had come upon him and Miranda on the porch swing. She was asleep in his arms. There was a huge bottle of Tanqueray gin perched precariously on the railing, and a tumbler sweating with melting ice at her feet.

Just before supper he had stood behind Beth's chair delivering a vigorous back rub, she moaning with the pleasure of it. My muscles were tense, too. I had gone outside and walked around until dinner was called.

Mathew Hazan was such a tireless, devoted, cultivated man. I wondered why I didn't like him more.

It seemed I wasn't the only one who was a bit stupefied by the evening meal. All bundled in sweaters against the evening chill, the group members were sitting around listlessly sipping decaf or after-dinner drinks, someone halfheartedly picking up a magazine now and then but soon abandoning it. Mat was still doing duty as spiritual guardian and cheerer-upper. I watched him drop down on cushions to "visit" with one lady and then the next, speaking quietly, joking, reassuring. It was amazing how much time he spent ministering to the needs of these women, but I supposed that as their manager that was his job. Still, there was only so much he could do.

Finally he said good night and climbed the

stairs, an outdated issue of *Opera News* tucked under his arm. This was my cue, my chance.

I lingered downstairs another ten minutes or so and then, surrendering Lulu to her rightful mistress, I too went up.

Mathew's door was ajar and there was a light on. I knocked gently and immediately heard his friendly "Come on in."

I closed the door behind me. He was lying across the bed, still fully clothed, his hands clasped behind his head.

"I'm sorry to disturb you," I said. "Might I talk to you for a few minutes?"

"Of course," he said. "Sit down." He smiled pleasantly at me, but as I was lowering myself into the straight-backed chair nearby, it was as though he were suddenly gripped by panic. He sat straight up. "There's nothing wrong, is there?"

"No, no. We're all fine."

I had to play this carefully, remembering to act the naïf.

"This is probably a very bad time to ask what I'm going to ask you," I began haltingly, "but I'll be going home shortly, and something Beth told me is so . . . interesting . . . that I just want to know a little more about it. I guess I could ask her, but . . . well, you know what shape she's in. . . ."

"Why don't you just ask?" he said. "Go ahead."

"Okay, I will. You see, Beth told me the quartet's here on a spiritual retreat. Which is a little difficult to understand. Because these women are . . . well, professionals. They aren't some church basement group on the run from a few bad notices in the European press."

"Hmm." He nodded. "Well, you couldn't be more right about their professionalism. But the truth is that I did bring us up here for a kind of spiritual renewal. Not to sound too hocus-pocus about it—I mean, I don't consider myself a guru or anything.

"But those reviews really *killed* us. It was quite a comedown after almost two decades of being one of the premier string quartets in the world— and they particularly loved us abroad.

"I guess Beth told you about the going over they gave us."

"Yes, she did," I said. "I was sorry to hear it."

"Let me tell you, it was brutal. Brutal! But you know, all that claptrap about our having lost our communal passion hit home in a strange way. The mesh was gone, and we knew it. And I knew we had to do something to get our chops back. It's been rough on everybody lately, but I had to do something."

There was a long silence. He unclasped his hands then and swung his feet around to the floor, staring hard at me as if trying to determine whether I understood the danger confronting the Riverside Quartet.

His voice became even more animated. "I *had* to do something for these women—my friends, my . . . It occurred to me to bring everybody all together in a kind of naked state, if you'll pardon the expression. To get at those things that seem to be tearing at us. And to make some sort of . . . primary contact with each other again. The way we once were. Friends. Comrades. What have you."

He stood up suddenly and brought the fist of one hand violently into the palm of the other. The movement startled me, and I sat back hard in my chair.

"But it was all a fantasy," Mat said bitterly. "Not only did I fail to pull everybody together— look at the horror that's happened up here. Will is dead. It was futile from the very beginning. All my fault. I had forgotten the way great string quartets are made. I guess I just ... forgot."

He sat down, calmer now. "You don't know what the hell I'm talking about now, do you?"

"Not really," I said.

"I'll try to explain. See, it used to be that groups like ours—chamber music groups, string quartets, whatever—were made up of musicians who realized they would never make it big as soloists on the concert stage. They accepted that they weren't individual giants—stars."

"Like Heifetz," I put in. "Or Jacqueline Dupré."

"Exactly," he said. "Like them. Well, musicians in groups like ours accepted that they would never fill Carnegie Hall to the rafters with people who'd paid top dollar to hear them and them alone. So they went along in their careers, playing well, even playing brilliantly in some cases, but playing with ... what? 'Modesty,' I think is the word. Good work, but without the panache of conceit. They didn't have the manner of the virtuoso.

"So you had a lot of fine, well-balanced string quartets around. And they were a big yawn.

"And then some genius asked himself: Why should a quartet mesh at the lowest level of energy? Why not come together at the highest level? What if each of the musicians in the quartet played and thought of herself as a virtuoso—why not let loose with all the panache and conceit the audience can handle?"

I couldn't help pricking him a little. "So you introduced a little show biz into the world of high culture. This unnamed quartet was the Riverside . . . and the genius was you."

"Right! It happened. And the quartet became a real musical force. Now, you must understand. There's no doubt that at first the Riverside was looked upon as some kind of cute novelty act—like an all-woman band from the Forties. And naturally, it didn't hurt that they were all pretty and smart and vibrant. It was all very sexy. Some even thought it was a kind of sop to the feminist movement, which was very strong in the Seventies. But what made the Riverside Quartet succeed and prosper and endure was the fact that each and every musician in the group was playing with an unfettered ego. As though she and she alone were the show the people had come to see. That was the secret of our success. Until now, that is.

"And of course, now we're in worse trouble than ever. No ridiculous little month in the country is going to get back what we had—that virtuosity, that fire. I guess I was underestimating how bad off we were. Or overestimating my own abilities. However you look at it, I made a horrible mistake dragging everyone up here. And my mistake cost Will his life."

"But how could you have known he was going to be killed?" I said calculatedly. "You can't blame yourself for that."

Hazan nodded slowly, silently thanking me for my words. He walked to the window then, and stared out into the blackness. The wind had picked up and was starting to rattle the panes.

"You're an actress?" he said quietly.

"That's right."

"Ah. That explains a lot."

"About what?"

"Most actors don't have a very high opinion of agents and managers. We always get the job done, but you think we're fools." He turned and looked directly at me. "You may be giving a decent enough performance, as far as it goes, but I don't believe for a moment that you came in here to get my opinion on spiritual retreats in the world of classical music."

I couldn't think of a reply. He had nailed me, stripped away my artifice.

"Why don't you just tell me what you really want?" he said, tapping on the desk with his nails.

I thought it best to go ahead and level with him. But what and how much should he be told of what I had already found out?

"I came into your room to ask for your opinion," I said, "but not about the retreat."

"About what, then?"

"Whether you think one of the members of the quartet could have murdered Will Gryder."

"Oh, please!" he said in disgust. "Jesus! Don't we have enough police crawling around?"

"I'm not with the police, Mr. Hazan."

"What is it then—morbid curiosity? More of your amateur detective nonsense?"

I kept my emotions in check. "Something like that."

"Well, here's my *opinion*, Miss Nestleton: There is no way—repeat, *no way*, *ever*—that anyone in this house could have killed Willy or had anything to do with such a crime. And anyone who thinks they could is just plain crazy. You obviously know nothing about Will Gryder and the affection we held him in.

"Will had his faults, he was only human. But he was the very best example of a musician. Understand? The music permeated his behavior. Sure, he was a show-off—but what performer isn't? And he may have been a little too wild and impulsive for his own good. But he was an honorable man, and extremely generous—yes, above all, generous. God knows how many musicians he helped out with money, jobs, putting them up at his apartment. And what about the lessons he taught at no charge? What about the hundreds of favors he did for people, never calling in the debts? No, he never became the great pianist he yearned to be, but he was a good musician and people respected him. You know what Glenn Gould once said? He said that if he *had* to listen to the romantic Russian composers, the only one he could bear was Willy Gryder!"

He paused there, staring at me in hostility. "You don't believe me, do you?"

I said nothing.

"So you think one of us murdered Will," he said scornfully. "Well, do me a favor, Miss Nestleton. Tell me why. Why would any of us want to kill him?"

"Jealousy," I said simply. "Rage. Passion."

"What do you mean—sex?"

"Yes."

"Are you ... but you *can't* be serious."

"Quite serious."

"Oh, for godsake, lady! Where are you from—
the farm? Listen, these women are sophisticated,
independent, grown-up people. They spend
three-quarters of the year on tour—away from
their homes and families. They get lonely—as
anyone would. And sure, some of them have
been to bed with Will Gryder. So what? He was
a grown-up, too—unmarried, and more than
willing to accommodate. Are you telling me one
of them was so hung up about a brief affair that
they would *kill* him? It's absurd!"

"It isn't absurd, Mr. Hazan. Will was murdered by someone intimately connected to him."

"Then maybe I should live in fear for my own
life!" he snorted.

"By that, do you mean you also have had af-
fairs with some members of this group?"

"Yes, if it's any of your business. I told you,
we're all friends. But I guess you really don't
understand that kind of friendship. You seem to
be stuck in some puritanical time warp."

"Jealousy is timeless, Mr. Hazan. And passion
can be that way, too."

"Bullshit!" he cried vehemently. His academic
veneer was peeling. I knew it was time for me to
leave.

"All right, Mr. Hazan. I think I've taken
enough of your time. And I'm sorry if I've upset
you." I rose and walked quickly toward the
door.

"Just a minute."

I turned back to him.

"I guess I owe you an apology, too," he said,
"in spite of the fact that you're insane to suspect

us. But I shouldn't have insulted you that way. I'm sorry."

"It doesn't matter."

"Oh, yes it does." He even laughed a little then. "But as long as you're so curious, and as long as your whole line of thought is so absurd, why don't you interrogate that nutty cook of ours? She's the one who hated Willy."

"Hated?"

"That's right. Willy just got on her nerves, always harassing her about the meals. He thought of himself as a gourmet, a culinary expert. But then he fancied himself an expert at everything. That's just the way he was. Other people might take it with a grain of salt, but it drove her crazy. He didn't mean anything by it, but she detested him."

"I see. Well . . ." I said tentatively, "I'll talk to her."

"Yes, you do that," he said, humoring me. "Who knows? Perhaps you'll be able to prove the butler did it—more or less."

I said coldly, "Good night, Mr. Hazan."

"Good night to you, Alice. But before you go, just tell me one more thing."

I paused, my hand on the doorknob.

"The way I understand it, you make a living changing kitty litter. So just tell me," he said. "Who the hell are you to go around interrogating us—about anything?"

I closed the door quietly behind me.

9

The alarm went off—low but abrasive. I reached under my pillow, where I had hidden the miniature clock, and searched wildly for the off button. It seemed to take forever to locate the right little switch; the damn thing went on buzzing and *brinngging* and chiming. Meanwhile, I kept the clock smothered by the pillow, fearing that the noise would wake Beth next door.

Finally I got the thing turned off. I vowed to fling the precious brass travel alarm clock and its black leather case into the creek first chance I got. It had been a gift from an old friend who'd passed through New York last year, her way of thanking me for showing her the town. At least it had done its job. I'd wanted to get up around six in the morning again in order to catch Mrs. Wallace alone in the kitchen.

As I was dressing, a funny image came to me: my scrappy, paranoid cat, Pancho, running from room to room. I was hit by a sudden wave of guilt at not having made a single call to Basillio or Mrs. Oshrin in New York. My poor kitties must have thought I'd abandoned them. I would call to check on them later in the morning, I decided. Right now I had to prepare myself for the talk with Mrs. Wallace. Talk, interview, interrogation . . . whatever one wanted to call it, I knew Mrs. Wallace would be a fairly tough nut to crack. She was stubborn and mercurial and shrewd, but I wasn't placing any bets that she'd killed Will Gryder just because of an argument over Hungarian goulash or the best way to roll pastry dough.

I sat on the edge of the bed to pull on my boots. I would have to be a little more careful in my dealings with *everyone* in the house. Mat Hazan had become very angry with me near the end of our conversation. *Who the hell are you?* He'd wanted to know what I thought I was doing, asking questions, investigating, snooping—who had given me the authority. No one had, of course. So I had to be more . . . well, if not circumspect, then certainly not confrontational, either. But then, Mathew Hazan had no idea that Roz and Ben and I had almost been killed—murdered—by some demonic puppeteer and his toy camel. Hazan had described Gryder's murder as a "horror," but obviously he didn't know even half the story.

The chirping of the birds on the tree limb outside my window had intensified. Between the birds outside and the dynasty of mice inside, if my two beasts were up here they'd probably think they'd died and gone to cat heaven. No stirrings from any of the other bedrooms, though. It was all quiet on the second floor. Then there came a faint thudding sound from below. It was a dull, rhythmic *chop chop chop*—at one and the same time familiar, frightening, and inevitable. Even though I knew in my head it had to be Mrs. Wallace doing something or other in the kitchen, my heart and intuition were saying that everyone in this old house was in danger of being murdered—*chop chop chop*—one by one, or two by two, or . . .

Oh, my. I had been in Massachusetts only for a few days and already I was slipping into a Lizzie Borden mode. I began to laugh at myself, and tried to remember the old bit of doggerel:

Lizzie Borden took an ax,
Gave her mother forty whacks.
When she found what she had done,
Gave her father forty-one.

Or something like that. I knew I didn't have the lines exactly right, but I was close enough. I remember thinking, as I walked down the stairs, that perhaps some perverse young playwright would one day do something interesting with the character of Lizzie Borden. I wouldn't mind being offered the lead in that one.

I had already rehearsed my opening line to Mrs. Wallace. I was going to say, oh so sweetly, "I've just been waiting for a chance to have another one of your scrumptuous omelets, Mrs. Wallace."

But when I walked into the kitchen to find her mercilessly severing the heads off countless bunches of turnips, carrots, and leeks, she announced immediately, "Not serving breakfast yet, dearie." I detected the slightest hint of a smirk at the corners of her mouth. "There's hot coffee if you want it," she added.

Mrs. Wallace was a tall, substantial woman, perhaps still on the near side of sixty. Obviously she had once been shapely, but her figure had broadened. She was wearing a hooded sweatshirt that read BERKSHIRE MUSIC FESTIVAL over a long housedress. On her feet were fur-lined, high-back slippers over thick woolen socks.

"Muffins'll be out in a minute," she said, the slightest bit placating. "You can have one of those if you're hungry."

I poured myself a cup of coffee and searched the table for sugar, settling for a packet of the brownish "natural" kind I sometimes saw in the supermarket. I stole a quick glance at the cook, who was still busy chopping and peeling.

How should I proceed? I had to follow up on Mat Hazan's comments about the cook's hatred for Will Gryder. But he might just have been making a sardonic joke. Suppose he was only getting back at me for my suspicions about the women in the quartet? Suppose he was simply trying to make a fool of me?

The coffee was delicious and warming. I decided on the direct approach. "I understand, Mrs. Wallace, that you and Will Gryder didn't get along," I said, stirring my drink.

"Is that what you understand, miss?" she retorted at once. "Now, what little birdy told you that?"

When I didn't answer she went back to her chopping, but she soon stopped, looking down at a potato she had already quartered.

"Well, the little birdy was right," she said after a minute. "We didn't get along in the least. Because he was a jackass. A troublemaker. The man complained about everything—*everything*.

He didn't like *this* soup, he didn't like *that* bread, the tenderloin was overdone, the duckling was too fatty, the coffee was too weak—not at all like they make it in *It-aly* . . . oh, nossir!"

She had started coring green and yellow peppers by then, heedlessly tossing their seedy innards around. So Mathew Hazan had not been joking: Will had made an enemy in Mrs. Wallace.

"Well," she went on, a bit more reflective now, "he was a handsome thing—I'll give him that. And those girls were crazy about him. Be sure of that. But that doesn't change what he was: a vain, arrogant, violent man. Like I said, a jackass."

The word *violent* jarred me. Miranda had said that Beth had been violent toward Will. But no one had characterized Will that way. Indeed, all I had heard about him seemed to call forth a pacific, pleasure-seeking man. Childish perhaps, willful perhaps, even promiscuous. But not violent.

I said as much to Mrs. Wallace, and asked, as gently as I could, if she was sure she wasn't exaggerating a bit.

"Exaggerating!" I'd obviously managed to offend her. "You don't know what happened here, dearie."

"Tell me in what way he was violent," I asked. "Exactly what did he do?"

She smiled ruefully and laid her paring knife aside.

"What would you say if I told you that on his second day here I saw him abusing Mr. Polikoff in the most terrible way?"

"And what way was that?"

"Why, he cursed poor Mr. Polikoff seven ways till sundown. And then he hit him across the face. Not once—three times—hard! And I saw it all. I was right here in this kitchen and they were out behind the storage shed."

"What were they arguing about?"

"Did I say they argued?"

"But they must have been quarreling about something if—"

"Look, missy, I'm telling you what I saw. Exactly what I saw. I don't know anything about an argument. I mind my own business."

It was an unexpected revelation. And an improbable story. I just didn't know what to make of it. But then, why would the woman lie?

Mrs. Wallace went in search of her favorite stew pot. I heard her humming under her breath. I finished my coffee and walked over to place my empty cup in the sink.

"Those muffins are ready now!" she called from the pantry, sounding like a dotty old granny in a TV ad.

"Thank you, no," I said.

"They're mighty good, dearie. Believe me."

"I'm sure they are, Mrs. Wallace. Thank you for the coffee."

I went into the still dark living room and sat in one of the big armchairs, drawing my legs up beneath me. I really hadn't had quite a full night's sleep. Before I knew it, I had fallen off.

A slammed door woke me. Mrs. Wallace had gone out. I sat up in the room, now quite light, with the sun struggling through the faded curtains. It was five minutes past eight. No one else had come down yet, but I could hear the shower going in one of the upstairs bathrooms.

The phone in the alcove was too inviting to resist. I sat down there fully intending to call Basillio in New York. But instead I dialed the local number I'd been given yesterday and stuck in the pocket of my jeans—Ford Donaldson's home phone.

After a few rings, a gruff voice came on the line. It didn't sound like Donaldson, but it was. I guessed that he was one of those bad morning risers who are difficult to deal with before they've had coffee and a shave.

"It's Alice Nestleton," I said softly. "Would you like me to call back later?"

"No. What can I do for you, Alice?"

I repeated exactly what Mrs. Wallace had told me about Will Gryder and the scene between him and Ben Polikoff.

There was a lengthy silence. I thought I heard some rustling noises. Was he getting out of bed now? Throwing on his clothes, excited by what I'd just said?

"Hello? Are you there, Ford?"

"Yes," he said distractedly. "Yes, I'm here." Then his tone became highly formal. "That was good information, good work. Thank you."

Another extended silence fell over the line. Just as I was about to speak, he said, "I see you're taking your part in this investigation very seriously." And again I heard muffled sounds and movement.

"You mean I'm taking it a bit *too* seriously," I said, becoming angry. "You really don't think what I told you has any value whatsoever."

"Not at all. It might turn out to be very valuable."

"Then what—" It was then that I distinctly heard another voice in the background, a woman's voice.

Oh, dear. Ford was in bed with someone. And I'd interrupted their early-morning revelry. I brought my thoughts back around in time to hear him saying something about the various elements of the case, and how I mustn't jump to any conclusions.

"I'm not saying one of them didn't do it, Alice. But there is something I want you to think about."

"What's that?" I asked.

"Remember Will Gryder's body when you discovered it. That chisel was driven deep into his chest. To do something like that requires a powerful hand. And it requires a tough and brutal nature—experience with violence, in other words. Now if Will had been *shot* to death, it would be a different ball game. It doesn't take a lot to pull a trigger—a little anger, a little too much to drink, maybe even a little curiosity. But to take a chisel and bury it in the breastplate of a living man—into a beating heart—well, do you see a violinist doing something like that, Alice? Or a gourmet cook?"

I wondered whether this gruesome disquisition had been offered to impress me or the lady at the other end. If this was the kind of pillow talk Lieutenant Donaldson enjoyed, he was even stranger than I'd initially thought.

"Well, thank you, Ford. That's all food for thought, indeed."

"Be in touch, Alice," he said, and hung up instantaneously.

I went back into the kitchen and helped myself to more coffee. I'd completely forgotten about calling Basillio. And I ate two muffins.

10

After that peculiar phone conversation with Ford Donaldson, I spent the remainder of the morning in a dreamy sort of state. It was almost as if I had determined to have some peaceful time in the country even if I had to steal it—even if I had to pretend that the awful things going on around the quartet weren't really happening.

I spent some enjoyable minutes watching Lulu the Scottish Fold cat, who was seated on one of the wide window ledges in the living room staring out at the birds. She was making tiny guttural noises, imitating their babble. I don't think it ever occurred to her that she was their natural enemy, their predator.

Watching cats watch something else has always been one of my pleasures. I have this rather eccentric belief that when you see a cat staring at something, say a bird in a tree, the cat has the ability to also see what has transpired to form the scene. In other words, not only is the cat seeing the bird in the tree at that instant, he is also capable of seeing the bird fly onto the branch, even though that happened in the past.

I once told my theory to a veterinarian. He laughingly counseled me to keep such views to myself, lest my friends conspire to place me in a psychiatric facility. Well, let the world scoff. I knew Lulu was seeing time past as well as time present as she looked out of the window. In fact, I know for certain that the reason cats are such spectacular hunters is simply that they can determine the direction of their prey's next move, since they have the power to see into the past and discover the direction of the prey's previous moves. Its gets kind of complicated from there, my theory. But no matter—Lulu didn't seem to give a damn about hunting, anyway.

Later in the morning I played the part of the audience while Darcy, seated at the piano, played backup for Beth, who was having great fun drinking Heineken from the bottle and belting out a medley of Bessie Smith songs.

"You wouldn't think a white lady from Denver could get down like this, would you?" Darcy said to me over her shoulder. "I bet you can sing too, Alice."

"Not me," I assured her. "I sound like a bag of rusty nails."

At one point Miranda drifted in and cattily requested her favorite Bessie tune: "If I Have to Play Second Fiddle, I Don't Want to Play at All."

Mathew Hazan dropped in after an hour session of weight-lifting in the attic. He drank Perrier from a quart bottle and entertained the group with some gossip about Zubin Mehta.

Then, just after lunch—rabbit stew, endive salad, key lime tart—Roz and Ben came home from the hospital.

As expected, the moment when the Polikoffs walked in was a happy one for the house. Roz and Ben were bruised but intact. There were two white gauze patches on Ben's face and one on his hand. Their friends and colleagues rushed forward to greet and welcome them home, hugs and kisses all around. I made not a move toward them.

I felt a palpable sense of danger emanating from the two of them, as if any vehicle they occupied at any time would call down upon it the wrath of some anonymous killer. In fact, my feelings for the two were so negative that I gathered Lulu up from the windowsill and held her fast, as a kind of psychic protection.

As I watched the circle of friends, I was struck by the passion of their interaction. Gone was the petty squabbling. Gone was all the tentativeness. For the first time I saw what was really there: four handsome, mature women at the peak of their creative lives who needed one another to perform, and two of their male associates who needed the women for their emotional and financial survival. I saw the Riverside String Quartet functioning in their mundane, everyday life as harmoniously as they did in their musical life.

Ben Polikoff was smiling at me. "It's nice to see you again, Alice. I'm so happy you're all right."

I dropped the cat back onto her perch and started to walk into the circle of friends. But I couldn't quite do it; I backed off. I still felt very much the intruder, the uninvited guest. I had a very chilling thought then: Could it be that Will Gryder had been murdered because he'd tried to penetrate this circle of intimacy? Had he taken some fatal liberty with this insular group of people? It was sobering to think so. I nodded pleasantly at Ben and sat down next to Lulu.

"I propose a celebration!" Mathew Hazan shouted joyfully. "A celebration because we've been reunited. And because it isn't every day our first violinist comes home from the hospital looking better than when she went in."

Roz leaned over and kissed Hazan's lips.

"You *are* up to this, aren't you, darling?" Ben asked her, sliding his hand around her tiny waist.

"Oh, phooey, Ben. Of course I am. Let's have some fun."

"Goody!" Miranda said. "Can we have a *terrible* party, Math—like in *Tender Is the Night*?"

"We'll come close," Hazan replied. "But we *are* still in Massachusetts, you know."

The house was buzzing with activity. Ben Polikoff waited until Mat was finished with his phone call to the liquor store and then cornered him.

"Maybe you ought to slow down a little, Mat. It's kind of short notice for a party, isn't it?"

"Nonsense!" Hazan said jauntily. "A party is a party. We'll rope in some of the crowd at Smith. And get that poet whatsisname who lives in the town. Miranda has some dancer friends in Lee who're probably sitting twirling their thumbs and would love to come out here. Whoever wants to come, will come."

Darcy sailed by at that moment and sent up a cheer at Hazan's words.

"We'll need some music," Hazan went on. "What should we do, Darcy?"

"Anything but rap!" Roz called as she climbed

the stairs. "I want there to be lots of dancing at this shindig."

"Reggae," said Beth, who had come through the room carrying a newly ironed white shirt. "Definitely reggae."

"Can we have just a few ballads?" Ben asked, succumbing to the festive spirit. "Coleman Hawkins, Ellington ... you know what I mean—a little 'Nearness of You' music." And he turned to place a playful hand on Mathew's head, saying, "You know how the pale moon excites *you*."

I remained by the window with my friend Lulu, apart, taking it all in. It took me a minute to realize that someone was addressing me.

"I'm sorry, Darcy. What did you say?"

"I said, do you need something to wear? I brought tons of clothes."

"Well, thank you. But I doubt they'd fit."

And suddenly the room was empty.

Except for me and Lulu and the little brown mouse who went flying by.

Beth and Darcy had made a quick run into town, to extend invitations to a few of the hip shopkeepers they knew and to pick up cassettes at the music store. They came back followed by the caterers, who would soon scandalize Mrs. Wallace with their unimaginative fare and skimpy portions. But at least now she had someone to order around. I had nothing to do, so I made myself scarce and goofed off with Lulu.

The house continued to be a hive of activity: furniture shuffled, vacuum cleaners going, the pinging of wine glasses and plates and silverware, manically cheerful phone calls, delivery boys at the back door, florists at the front. The energy seemed almost pathological.

And then, at five-fifteen, the first guests arrived: twins. Two young women musicians from the music department at Smith. After them, the old poet who lived in the town of Covington, a benign-looking white-haired gentleman. Then a South American pianist, and a professor of English literature whose controversial book on Emily Dickinson had recently been published. After that, a renowned geneticist in Rastafarian braids. Two candle-makers—a married couple—and three gaunt modern dancers. And so it went.

They had all come on short notice. Was it the prestige of being hosted by the Riverside Quartet that had brought them out? Or the notoriety of the murder, which had been in all the local papers? Or just escape from the routine of rural life? I couldn't tell, but they were all there, and others kept coming, and soon the stately house was alive with people eating and drinking and arguing good-naturedly between dances.

From time to time as the party progressed, one or another of the women in the quartet would come over and playfully condemn me as a wallflower. I would always smile and claim fatigue, but the label fit all too well that night. Once or twice I crossed Mathew Hazan's path, but he didn't speak to me at all. I felt alone and unnecessary, and unsociable. Even so, at one point I found myself being swept onto the dance floor by a persistent sculptor who lived up the road. He stationed us next to Beth and the young man she'd been dancing with for some time, a performance artist who moonlighted as the projectionist at the movie house in Northampton. By the time the song had ended I was a little overheated, and I asked Beth if the two of us might repair to our drinks over on the window seat, where Lulu waited.

Beth took a healthy swig of her screwdriver. "What do you think, Alice? He's sort of hot, isn't he?"

"Excuse me?"

"*Him*, Alice. The one I was dancing with. Great forearms, don't you think?"

Rather than answer her, I decided to jump in with some questions of my own. "Listen, Beth, speaking of . . . forearms, were you having an affair with Will Gryder?"

My words seemed to stun her. She stiffened visibly. But then she recovered and turned on a blinding smile. "Oh, Alice, you should know better than to listen to rumors. Who told you that—Roz?"

When I made no reply, she smiled even more brightly. "Listen, dear, never believe what the first violinist says about the second violinist."

"It wasn't Roz."

"Well, then, I suppose it's Miranda who's been spouting off. Hell, cellists are even crazier than violinists. They live for drama—especially that one." Beth nodded toward Miranda, who stood across the room in a beaded black jersey catsuit and knife-point high heels, laughing loudly as an intense Danish philosopher held forth.

"Did you know, for instance," Beth raced on, "that Miranda never recovered from the revelation that she wasn't Piatigorski?" Beth laughed uproariously at her own line. "Did you ever see him perform, by the way?"

"No."

"God! You should have. He was an immense man who used to stride on stage carrying his cello over his head like a warrior—like an attacking Indian. Miranda's wanted to do that all her life, but she's never had the gumption. She just talks a mighty good game." Then Beth seemed to become lost in her thoughts.

"Sorry to press you, Beth, but I have a good reason for wanting to know: Did you and Will Gryder make love in one of the sheds by the creek?"

She looked at me over the rim of her glass before answering, slowly, "Yes. And in a few other places over the years. Satisfied?"

"Not entirely. I'd like to ask about a couple of other things."

She laughed in astonishment. "You are something else, Alice. Okay, go ahead."

"Did you quarrel with him after you made love . . . a few days before he was killed?"

"We had a beauty of a fight that day, yes. But it was soon forgotten. Will and I were very, very close. We loved each other, but we also sometimes hated each other. And we fought like cats and dogs over the damnedest things—or over nothing. We were just that way. The anger never lasted because . . . well, because we were so much a part of each other. Oh, I don't mean the sex. It was all right, but the truth is, Willy was nothing to write home about as a lover. In fact, I always thought he might have been secretly gay. I think he looked at sex with women as another way to be mothered. He was a man who needed a lot of mothering. He was so vulnerable and—"

Beth stopped suddenly. "Oh, wow! Wait a minute. Oh, Alice! Sweet, surprising little Alice! You think I *killed* him, don't you?"

I continued to look at her.

"I *didn't* kill him, Alice!" She had spoken quite loudly, and we both glanced around to see if anyone was noticing us. "I didn't!" she said more softly. "How could I? Will was my friend. He loved me. He even gave me Lulu—when she was just a kitten."

Again this profile of Will Gryder as a gentle soul. To counter it, I described to her his attack on Benjamin Polikoff, exactly as Mrs. Wallace had reported it to me. The glass in Beth's hand began to tip over. I took it from her and set it on the windowsill. The story had unnerved her, apparently. She went pale. Or was it the alcohol that explained that?

"Look here," she said a moment later. "I don't know why you're so interested in us, but if you're going to pry you should at least get your stories straight. Mrs. Wallace must be a nut job to say a thing like that. Those things she said about Will are simply not true. And she should realize what an awful, irresponsible thing it is to spread rumors like that after someone has been . . . *Will* has been . . . murdered.

"If you must know, there is an old secret involving Will and Ben. Only I guess it isn't much of a secret. Will and Roz had an affair a few years ago. A pretty heavy one. She even left Ben briefly. But that's all in the past. She went back to her husband and Will went on to somebody else—or lots of somebodies. And all of us became friends again. That's the way it's always been with us, Alice. With all of us. We keep our priorities straight. We're ... grown-ups."

Beth was the second member of the group to remind me of the prerogatives of adulthood. I didn't know whose lecture I found more silly—hers or Mat Hazan's.

"You do believe me, don't you, Alice?" Beth said fervently. "About Willy ... and about me. I swear none of us would ever hurt him." Beth pressed my hand tightly, and when I merely pressed hers back, saying nothing, she picked up her glass and moved off.

So it was *Roz* and Will now. In addition to Ben and Will. In addition to Beth and Will. In addition to ... what? It was hard to think with all the noise. I saw the young sculptor wave at me. I immediately ran for cover.

11

The party should have been over, or at least on its last legs. It was past ten in the evening. But new blood had arrived in the form of three people—two men and a woman—whom everyone seemed to be making a terrible fuss over. I was too weary to inquire who they were.

Lulu was nowhere to be seen. I hoped she was finally tracking down field mice as Nature intended.

I couldn't bear that seat in the window another minute. When the crowd rushed forward in adoration of the newly arrived trio, I saw my chance to leave the party and call Tony. If I wasn't mistaken, this was one of the nights he'd be staying with my cats in the apartment.

There was only one telephone on the second floor and it was on a low table in the hallway, just outside the Polikoffs' room. I sat down cross-legged on the worn carpet, took the phone into my lap, and dialed my own number in New York. Tony answered on the third ring.

"Well, stranger, it's about time," he said.

"I've been bad about keeping in touch, Tony. I'm sorry. Is everything okay there?"

"Everybody's fine. Except you're interrupting a rehearsal of my new play. Bushy is appearing in the Stanley Kowalski-type role. I'm the aging female lead. And Pancho is directing—when I can find him."

"Are they eating?"

"At every conceivable opportunity."

"Do they miss me?"

"What are you, kidding? They lapsed into horrendous feline depression the day after you left. I've had to put the pair of them on antidepressants. Matter of fact, we're all on them."

"Any messages?"

"Yeah. Your agent called. Said not to worry about the *Beast* review, that everybody knows that critic is demented."

"He happens to be an excellent reviewer, Tony."

"Okay, Swede. Be a martyr. Let's not call him demented. Let's just say he's a man who plays badminton every Tuesday and Thursday."

"What the hell does that mean?"

"Nothing, really. Just making conversation. It's good to hear from you, Swede. I miss you, no kidding. What's going on up there?"

"Well, it's cold."

"Invite me up. I'll get you warm."

I didn't answer.

"So what's the story up there—really? You sound strange."

"Do I? In what way?"

"You know—you've got that abstracted kind of sound. Which usually means the hunt is on. . . . Hey, Swede, are you okay?"

"I'm quite all right. But there *has* been some trouble up here."

"Oh, shit. What?"

"Let me call you tomorrow, Tony. I don't have time to explain it all now."

I hung up after convincing Basillio that I really was all right. I sat listening to the sounds of merriment downstairs. The party was still flying. And I was still alone upstairs.

All alone. That fact suddenly intrigued me. At the end of the hall, up a few steps, was the bedroom Will Gryder had stayed in. It was possible, I realized, for me to go in and have a look around, and no one would ever know. And what would I be looking for? I had no idea. It was just something that ought to be done. No doubt about that. It wasn't even illegal—just a bit illicit.

I climbed the two stairs quietly and entered the room, which had one of those dramatically slanted ceilings. For a tall person like me, the exposed beams posed a danger of major concussion. As I stooped a bit to avoid that danger, it occurred to me that the more removed you were from the center of the Riverside Quartet the further down the hall you slept. Will had been an occasional guest artist and accompanist, so it figured that he'd had this quiet little room. I suppose they'd have assigned it to me if he hadn't been in residence when I arrived.

I closed the creaky door to hide my trespassing and felt my way in the dark till I found the old wall lamp I'd sighted a moment before. When I flicked the light on it sent an eerie glow through the room—which was a mess.

The mess was understandable: According to Ford Donaldson, someone had rifled the room and then the police had searched it again. There was one outsized dresser in the corner. Each of its six drawers were open, the edges of clothing sticking out. Other clothes were scattered on the bed and the floor, but a jarringly modern clothes stand held a suit jacket neatly waiting for its owner, who of course would never again wear it. There were other things obviously preserved exactly as Will had left them the evening he'd walked out of this room for the last time: an uncapped fountain pen on the headboard, three books stacked on the small, rough-hewn bed table, and several booklets of sheet music on the pillow.

I looked through the books. One of them was in fact not a book but a copy of *The Massachusetts Review*, a literary journal. The issue was a couple of years old, and, oddly enough, the list of contributors on the back cover included the name Will Gryder. I turned to his piece and took ten minutes to skim my way through it. It turned out to be a decently enough crafted short story, one of those adolescent betrayal tales focusing on the father. Here was yet another aspect of the victim I hadn't known about: He'd had literary aspirations.

I glanced at the sheet music long enough to see that all three were by Chopin—two sonatas and a mazurka. I didn't examine it further, for I can't read a note of music.

Then I went through all the drawers. Will had brought along more underwear for his vacation up here than most men owned. Next I moved on to the old armoire, a knotty pine thing with splinters galore, just waiting to jab the uninitiated. Inside was an expensive London-tailored suit, a sports jacket, three shirts, and a windbreaker. I searched every pocket. Nothing there.

At the bottom of the armoire were three pairs of shoes. I tried to recall what kind of shoes he had been wearing when we found his body, but I couldn't. One of the pairs were old sneakers; then there were suede chukka boots; and finally a pair of black dress shoes. The moment my fingers went inside the black shoes I felt a surge of excitement. There was paper inside. A hiding place for something important? Something the unknown searcher and the state police had missed? I pulled out the rolled-up newspaper, feeling utterly stupid. Will Gryder had simply stuffed his shoes with newspapers to help them keep their shape—as many well-brought-up children are taught to do. Disgusted, I pushed the shoes back and closed the armoire door. At least I had avoided the splinters.

There was a little bathroom at the rear of the room, without a door. An old-fashioned wash basin was visible from where I stood, and a leather toiletry case lay unzipped on top of it. I went in and picked through the completely anonymous items in the case: toothbrush, disposable razors, nail clip, condom.

I walked slowly back to the small bed then, sat down, and stared around me. As I looked down at the sheet music on Will Gryder's pillow, I began to feel, for the first time, the full weight of his death, a man I had never met. I felt the sheer, inexplicable sadness of it all. And for some reason I thought of something one of my acting coaches had once told me. He had been an excellent teacher, weaning me away from the Method, but he was prone to making murky philosophical pronouncements and he suffered from recurrent bouts of crippling depression.

He'd told me once that he was obsessed with a comment of Camus. To paraphrase it: No matter how perfect a society human beings construct, there will always be trolley car accidents in which young children are killed.

That's what I thought about as I sat in that dead, attic-like room, a steady cold rain pattering against the little blacked-out window near the ceiling. I had found nothing in the room. I had trespassed and found nothing. That was a very bad sign.

12

Breakfast at eleven! That sounds pretty decadent for a weekday. But this was the morning after the impromptu party, and no one, other than Mrs. Wallace, had stirred before ten.

Mat Hazan had gone out for a morning jog, and the bruised Benjamin Polikoff was still soaking his weary limbs in the tub. It was girls only at the table, and we must have looked like a group photo from a day camp for retired chorines.

Breakfast was plentiful and soothing: hot cereal with heavy sweet cream, raspberries, fresh-baked biscuits, newly squeezed orange juice with plenty of pulp, eggs baked with cheese and tomatoes, savory country sausage.

The ladies were all hung-over and tired from the party, but the group seemed for the first time to have broken free from the shock that the violent death of their friend had induced. They had grieved, and would grieve. But the party had somehow pointed them in another direction—toward the future.

Of course, they didn't know that another murder had almost occurred, in the Mercedes. Perhaps knowing that might have kept their grief alive a bit longer. On the other hand, one of them *had* to know about the rigged car accident, because he or she had been responsible for it.

I watched them closely as they ate breakfast. I listened to them carefully as they bantered at the table, remarking on incidents from the party and teasing each other in the way sober adults tend to do after a night of uncommon drinking. It was hard to believe that one of these people had driven the chisel into Will Gryder's chest. Harder still to believe he or she would gladly have exterminated three of us at one blow, even if only one of the occupants of the car was a danger to that person.

Motive? It seemed that many of these people had some petty reason for disliking or resenting the late pianist. But a negligible motive doesn't usually result in a stake through the heart. I grimaced, thinking about "motives." My friend Detective Rothwax used to tell me that motives are meaningless; that motives are ridiculous; that good homicide detectives ignore the concept of "motive" completely. They want to know how the murder was committed, when, and by whom. They want every bit of crime-scene evidence they can suck up, but motive means nothing to them. It's a luxury they can't afford.

Rothwax used to tell any one of a dozen stories to illustrate his point. He particularly liked the one about the sociopath who has just been released from prison after serving eight years. He goes into a bar and gets drunk. The bartender eventually throws him out. On the street, he follows a man who he feels has insulted him. He picks up a thick wooden slat and brains the man, killing him instantly. He's walking away from the corpse when he realizes he may as well take any valuables that may be on the body, so he empties the poor man's pockets. The next day the newspapers report the murder and claim the man was killed during an attempted robbery. Point, set, match.

But Rothwax's world was not my world. I collected motives. I needed motives—big ones and small ones.

I snapped out of my somber thoughts about the complexities of motive just in time to hear Darcy scolding her colleagues in a mock-serious voice: "We all behaved very badly last night, ladies."

"Whatever it is you're referring to, Darcy dear, I'm sure we're guilty as charged," Roz said happily.

"I mean, *very* badly," Darcy reiterated.

"Don't get too carried away," Beth cautioned. "I doubt we did anything that terrible."

Darcy, her mouth full of raspberries, said, "Oh yes, we did! We didn't drink a single toast to Aunt Sarah!"

A collective groan went up from the assembled. I didn't understand a thing, and it must have shown on my face.

"We're being a little rude, people," Beth admonished them all. "Alice doesn't know what we're talking about." And then she leaned in to me and explained: "Aunt Sarah was Roz's aunt. She's the one who gave us the seed money we needed to get started as a group—fifteen thousand dollars—to buy clothes, rent halls, buy ad space, everything. She underwrote our first tour, which was New England, by the way, so she's sort of our patron saint."

Miranda lifted her coffee mug high and intoned, "To Sarah, who was there when we needed her most." Everybody drank to Aunt Sarah.

"Has Aunt Sarah passed away?" I inquired.

"Yes," Roz told me, "several years ago. And we don't honor her the way we used to. A shame."

Ben and Mat joined the table then. Not that they were responsible for the ensuing dissension, but soon after they sat down the conversation did turn acrimonious. Some members of the group wanted to abort the "retreat," given the circumstances, and go back to New York. I listened for a while to their arguing, which seemed to result in a complete deadlock, and then, feeling very ill at ease, I left the table, grabbed the heavy coat I'd adopted, and walked outside.

I walked to my rented car, climbed in, and ran the engine for a few minutes. I had been thinking of driving into Northampton alone, but then I thought better of it and decided instead to take a walk over to the sheds and pay a visit to my rocking friend, the toy camel. I gave Will's studio extremely wide berth this time, frightened that I'd hear that music again. I was in no mood for occult experiences.

My friend was right there on top of the cartons. Soulful as ever. I reached up and set him rocking. "Nice to see you again, you murderous dromedary," I whispered. And it *was* good to see him. He was something concrete—visible, tangible evidence of the murder attempt. Well, maybe not to anybody but me. But at the very least he signaled the existence of a mad person somewhere in the vicinity, who thought it was fun to wreck moving vehicles.

It was a little too raw in the shed to carry on an extended petting session with the stuffed beast. I stilled his rocking and started to leave. Obviously, I could come back and see him anytime I liked—he was going nowhere. And that suddenly struck me as very peculiar. If the camel really had been part of a murder attempt, why had the guilty party left it there in the shed for just anybody to find? Sure, the door to the shed was always closed, but it was easy for anyone to get in. The local kids did it all the time, according to Lieutenant Donaldson.

If I'd been the one who'd caused a near-fatal wreck using the camel, I most certainly would have hidden it—buried it, burned it, given it to an orphanage, anything. Unless, of course, Ford Donaldson was right and it was just my delusion that the toy had been used to cause the accident. But I knew, all his logical objections aside, that Ford was *not* right, that someone *had* tried to kill the occupants of that Mercedes, me included, even if I was just an afterthought, a wild card.

So why did he leave the damn thing here, more or less in plain sight? Maybe the man—or woman—was simply a fool. Many murderers are. Surely that's why they're caught.

Was the camel's master just careless, sloppy?

Or was it quite the opposite? Perhaps the individual was wise rather than foolish, fastidious rather than careless. Perhaps the camel had been placed here on purpose, even methodologically, as in the "purloined letter" ruse. That old saw from the Poe story seemed to be timeless: If you want to hide something, place it in plain view.

I thought of all the futile searches that had

been made of Will Gryder's room: the killer's, the law's, and mine. What if Will *did* have something in his room he wanted to hide? What if he knew the room might be searched, and so used the same purloined-letter procedure as the would-be killer who had "hidden" the toy camel?

If any of that was true, I already knew exactly what constituted the purloined letter in this case: three booklets of sheet music, all by Chopin. Two sonatas that looked mighty daunting, and a "mazurka," whatever that was, lay right out in the open, on Will Gryder's pillow.

They were still arguing when I walked into the house. They either didn't know or didn't care that I'd returned. Or perhaps they had never noticed that I'd left. I walked quickly upstairs without removing my coat. The moment I hit the second-floor landing I rose on my toes and moved along the wall until I was inside Will's room.

The music was exactly where I'd last seen it.

In the first booklet, two pages from the end, was a small, tissue-thin envelope, the kind you sometimes get at the post office when you purchase stamps. It wasn't even sealed. In the middle of the second booklet, there was an identical envelope. The third piece of music held some sheets of onionskin paper, not in an envelope at all but simply tucked in between sheets of music. My heart was beating like a drum. I had unpurloined the purloined letter.

I slipped everything I'd found up my sleeve and walked back to my room, locking the door behind me. Sitting on my narrow bed, I opened the first envelope with hands that were just slightly trembling.

Inside the first envelope was a photograph of each of the members of the Riverside String Quartet, all taken when the women were much younger. Their clothing and hairstyles made it a pretty good bet that the shots had been taken during the early 1970s, or maybe even a bit earlier, the late 1960s.

The second envelope contained a computer disk. That was all.

The two folded sheets from the last piece of music turned out to be badly water-damaged. They appeared to me to be some kind of genealogy, or breeding chart—of the kind one might see for thoroughbred racehorses, tracing sires and dams back several generations to the foundation stock. But nearly all the names on the paper had faded, washed away, and the only visible marks left were the lines that apparently signified the branching—like tree limbs—from one generation to the next.

At the top of each sheet some lettering was visible—visible but cryptic. The first sheet was headed by the word SUZY in capital letters. The second carried the heading BRIT.

None of it meant a damn thing to me. I was furious, disappointed, and swept the whole pile to one side, very nearly onto the floor. Then, a little embarrassed by my own petulance, I gathered the material and neatly reassembled it as I had found it. And then I placed it all *under* my pillow. Will Gryder had left it all on top of his pillow, but he knew exactly what these mystifying documents meant. And he was dead.

13

"Why so sad?" Beth asked me.

The others seated at the dining table for our evening meal all turned toward me, faces clouded with fake concern.

"It's nothing," I said, smiling wanly. But I *was* sad, and tired, and distracted. Why shouldn't I be? I had spent the last few hours again and again picking through the things I'd found in Will's room, trying to understand what the items meant, either separately or together.

"She just misses the big city," Darcy said. "Some of us is country girls, and some of us just ain't."

I did chuckle a bit at that. I had no intention of telling her I'd been raised on a farm.

"Well," Mathew Hazan noted, "she may miss the bright lights, but she certainly couldn't find better food anywhere in Manhattan." He seemed to have half forgiven me for my prying suspicions. Mat passed me the cruet of Mrs. Wallace's special blue-cheese dressing. He was right about the food: It was the best salad dressing I'd ever tasted.

The cook was serving up "Americana" that night, saluting the basic corn-fed goodness of the heartland. The salad was fantastic. Then came an enormous lean brisket, sliced paper-thin and served with garlicy little potatoes and glazed carrots.

By the time Mrs. Wallace was clearing the plates from the main course, the wind outside had begun to howl. Someone had put on an old recording of the Riverside String Quartet performing Beethoven's opus 59, no. 3, done some years ago in Germany. I got up to raise the volume ever so slightly, and used that as an excuse to look at the worn album cover, which featured a photograph of the women in the recording studio. Yes, they all looked young and fresh, but this photo wasn't from exactly the same period as the snapshots I'd discovered in Will's room.

The cook reentered with her tray, and set before each of us a dish of stewed plums. Stewed plums—talk about comfort food! The meal had been so simple and delicious, I found myself wondering whether difficult Mrs. Wallace was really some renowned gourmet chef, moonlighting during her vacation to raise enough money for daily psychiatric care.

The only problem of any note, as we all turned our attention to the lemon meringue pie and coffee, was that Roz had dropped her spoon on the floor. Ben put such frenzied effort into retrieving it that Roz, obviously embarrassed, said to the rest of us: "He has this knack for making me feel like a baby in a high chair."

Beth laughed wickedly. "But that's how you prefer it, I always thought."

Roz's otherworldly blue eyes flashed. And for a moment it seemed as if she really had the power to call the wrath of the gods down upon Beth's head.

"Nice work, Beeswax," Miranda said through her teeth.

I saw then that Beth genuinely regretted her remark. There were tears in her eyes. She jumped out of her seat and fairly ran to Roz's side. "I'm sorry, sweetie. Please forgive me." And she kissed the part in Roz's hair.

Roz swallowed hard. "It's all right, Beeswax. Just sit down. . . . You, too, Ben . . . please!" He had been standing nearby, the spoon dangling foolishly from his fingers.

As I ate my dessert I surreptitiously watched each of the women, matching them in my mind with the old photos. Had each given Will a photo of herself? And why? Why had he packaged them like so many baseball cards in a little boy's prized collection?

There was no more talk for a long time. We sat listening to the music. These women had the uncanny ability to suddenly tune out the world—not to mention the ability to make the nonmusical guest feel like the fifth wheel. The record ended. Mrs. Wallace brought in more coffee and placed a bottle of Grand Marnier on the table. Most of the women looked at it with distaste—they'd drunk their limit the night before. Only Mat and Miranda helped themselves.

"Mrs. Wallace," Darcy called out before the cook had swung back through the doorway, "were those fresh plums that you stewed?"

"Of course they were."

"But where did you get them this time of year?"

"Darcy, you can get fresh anything if you know where to shop," Roz chided. "I believe

Mat when he says your cooking tastes like old sweatbands."

Darcy waved away the comment and then spoke directly to Beth. "Would your cat eat plums?"

"Lulu? I doubt it. She might play with a plum, though."

Miranda said testily, "That's about all she could do, play with fruit. She's obviously afraid of mice."

They all laughed.

Ben then added: "There are so many mice in this house now, they've started their own orchestra."

Mat picked up on the humor. "*And* a ballet company," he said. "Last night I saw them do *Swan Lake* with a full corps."

Beth reached across the table and patted Hazan's hand. "Be patient. Lulu will start to hunt soon, I assure you. She just needs a little time to acclimate."

"That's nonsense, Beth," Miranda said analytically, through the clouds of her cigarette smoke. "Your cat may be pretty, but let's face facts: She's a spoiled little house cat." Then she sat back and said expansively, as if sharing her new theory of evolution with the world, "Besides, that breed are simply not good mousers."

Her manner irritated me no end. I put my two cents in. "I think the Scottish Fold breed is near the top of the line when it comes to mousing—usually, that is. After all, they're basically farm cats. The line of cats that eventually produced the Scottish Fold earned their keep for hundreds of years on farms. So it stands to reason."

Miranda exploded in fury—anger so fierce

that I instinctively raised a hand to my face as if to block a blow. "Who are you, the feline pope?" she screamed. "Who do you think you are to instruct us about anything? You ridiculous, snooping fool! Roz and I were working in the most exclusive cat shops in Manhattan while you were— Oh, why don't you just get into your cheap little car and go home!"

No one said a word. Beth couldn't bring herself to look at me, though she tried. Miranda, who had gone chalk-white, seemed pinned to her chair, the coffee cup in her hand frozen in time and space.

When I was able to rise, I excused myself and walked grimly upstairs. I entered my small room, closed the door, and lay down heavily on the bed. It had been a long time since I'd felt so humiliated. I was also frightened, in some unvoiceable way.

But Miranda had asked a good question. Why *didn't* I just get into my rental car and drive away from here? This was no vacation, no rural interlude to cure my wounded feelings over a bad review. Why was I dabbling in a murder when my help was not wanted—not by the victim's friends, and not by the police? Why was I still enraged by an automobile accident in which no one had been seriously hurt, and which, though I believed it to have been a murder attempt, the professionals considered only a skid on a wet road caused by a farm dog? And even if it was a murder attempt, surely Roz or Ben had been the intended target. It could have nothing to do with me—I was the stranger here. But for some crazy reason, I seemed to think of myself as the personal one-woman security force for the Riverside String Quartet. When and where had I been given that responsibility?

And why did these people dislike me so much? Was it because they knew I was investigating the murder? It had to be that. People usually like me. Particularly women my own age. Particularly other theater people—and musicians, like it or not, are theater people, performers, just like actors.

What was the matter with that crazy woman Miranda? What had I said to incur her wrath? Nothing. I had made a few mundane remarks about a breed of cats.

I turned toward the wall—a distinctly childish thing to do, almost primal. This house was making me regress into childhood. My loneliness had that helpless, aching quality to it.

I heard a noise outside my door. I tensed. The house was also making a nervous wreck of me. Was someone spying on me now? Or perhaps it was Beth, too ashamed to knock.

I strode silently, quickly across the floor and opened the door suddenly to catch the intruder.

It was only Lulu. Looking up tenderly at me.

"Come on in, kitty," I said. "The company down there isn't very pleasant, is it? No wonder you can't catch any mice." I took her in my arms and sat down on the bed with her. We were both fugitives from Miranda's ire.

Why was I so frightened by that ire? I had probably been chewed out worse in drama class. Maybe it was because she had been the first of the group to exhibit the kind of rage that might propel a chisel into a man's chest. Ford Donaldson had said that this kind of murder requires a special kind of violence, and a special kind of strength.

I picked up Lulu and dangled her in front of me for a moment, looking at her lovely face framed by those lovelier ears. "Did what I said about your ancestors offend you, my pet? No, of course not." So why should it so upset Miranda Bly? I was beginning to feel very uneasy about the whole episode, as if I had stumbled upon something ugly.

I placed the cat on the floor and she amused herself by playing with my shoelace.

God, I was beginning to hate them all—their formal dinners, their self-involvement, their terrible tempers, and above all their almighty talent, which they seemed to think gave them a kind of superiority over the rest of the world.

Why didn't I just leave? They wanted me out. Why didn't I stay somewhere else in the area? I knew why. Because the hunt was more important than the hurt.

"All I said," I told Lulu in a hushed voice, "was that you Scottish guys are great mousers. Except for you, you little aberration. . . . You're just a little aberration, aren't you?"

What did I know about Scottish Fold cats, anyway? Just facts I'd picked up here and there. I knew that they had originated as a spontaneous mutation in Scottish farm cats in the 1960s. I knew they had become very popular in the U.S. in the early seventies, even though the influential cat-breeder associations had refused to recognize them as a breed. I knew the breed was established by outcrossing to British and American shorthairs. I remembered reading that all these cats traced their folded-ear trait to a single cat. And that the color range of Scottish Folds was expanding rapidly, as well as the range of fold on the ears. Certainly I knew they were all, even the ones in litters whose ears did not fold, adorable. And I knew that they all had those beautiful golden eyes. Or did they?

Why couldn't I remember that mythical foundress of the line? I definitely remembered laughing when I'd first heard about her, amused that there was an identifiable first lady of the Scottish Folds. There was something so refreshing about it. After all, no one could name the first man or woman to use fire. Or the first domesticated horse. But there really was one lady whom the whole world knew as the first folded-ear cat.

If only I could have asked Lulu for the name of her great-great-great grandmother. I knew it was something simple and honest, like Betty, or Stella, or . . . *Susan*—was that it? Not Susan, Suzy! *That* was the name of the primeval Scottish Fold cat—the foundress.

Suzy! I began to tunnel feverishly under my pillow. There at the top of one of the papers from Will's room was the name, the heading on a faded family tree. Was I looking at a feline breeding chart compiled some time in the past, where I would find the foundation cat still perched on the top branch of the tree, where not enough generations had gone by to relegate Suzy to the mythical realm she now inhabited?

I looked desperately, hopefully, at the second sheet of paper. The letters at the top of that one spelled out BRIT. Could this one be a breeding chart of the British short-haired cats used to establish the Scottish breed by outcrossing?

I sent up a whoop of triumph, and then clamped my hands to my mouth, afraid the sound might have traveled down to the group. But I heard no footsteps on the stairs.

I picked up the computer disk from Will Gryder's stash, praying that it contained the secret of the charts.

I needed help! On several fronts. And I knew just who I'd turn to for starters. But that would have to wait until morning. I was exhilarated, and just as exhausted. Yes, morning would come soon enough. It even comes after you're dead, as my grandmother, in one of her darker moods, had once observed.

14

By seven-thirty the next morning I was in a phone booth in Northampton, at a little espresso place fitted out to pass for a coffee bar in Paris.

I was placing a collect call to John Cerise in Glen Rock, New Jersey. John has nothing to do with either the theater or the music worlds. He's a cat man, pure and simple. We met years ago when I first started cat-sitting for a rich lady on Central Park South whose passion was English shorthairs. Cerise was then, as he is now, a cat show judge and breeder, whose love for felines is proverbial. We rarely speak to each other more than twice a year, but there is a genuine affection between us. He also has a special spot in his heart for my crazy cat Pancho, who, John once said, is the reincarnation of one of Napoleon's marshals.

In his sixties now and extremely well preserved, John has the reputation of being a dandy. He always looks exotic, with his slicked-back ebony hair and, in summer, his elegant white linen suits. He is an ageless relic from another time and place. And it is very fitting that he is a cat man. He seems perfectly and easily androgynous. He exudes a kind of cool sensuality that is quite pleasing to be around, although one can rarely identify the objects of his passion. It is John Cerise I always call when I need feline information of any kind, particularly in matters criminal.

The phone on the other end kept ringing and ringing. I counted fourteen rings before the dazed voice answered. I knew I'd be waking him. But he accepted the collect call gladly.

It was too early to make small talk. As soon as I greeted him I asked for my favor: Could he spend a few hours making calls and gathering information for me? I needed to know more about the Scottish Fold cats. About the breeding and buying and selling of them in the New York area during the 1970s.

"What a strange request, Alice," he said. Then he laughed, and added, "Well, I didn't have much planned for today, anyway. And I'm not even going to ask you why you need this information, my dear. I know better." I gave him the phone number at the Covington Center. He told me he'd call about seven that evening.

I hung up and dialed my friend Amanda's number. She lived in a cottage outside Northampton and taught at Smith. At least I had thought she still taught there, but when I reached her and offered to meet her before her first class, she told me she was on a year's involuntary hiatus and was supporting herself doing free-lance work. Amanda was bowled over when she heard I was calling from Northampton, only fifteen minutes away by car.

"What are you doing up here?" she asked. It was Amanda, of course, who'd gotten me the lecturing assignment at Smith all those years ago. We still exchange postcards from time to time.

"Just took a drive up to visit another friend," I half lied.

"Well, get over here immediately!"

Her renovated cottage looked exactly the same as the last time I'd visited. So did Amanda: a small, strong-featured woman with close-cropped ringlets of gray hair. Her hair had turned irretrievably gray when she was in her early thirties, and that suited her just fine. She dressed like a bohemian sculptor, always sporting mile-long scarves or mufflers and thick, vengeful sandals. Her house was filled to bursting with books, thousands of them. And it seemed that at least half of them had to do with one aspect or another of Virginia Woolf and her times. What Amanda seemed to have done with her portion of passion in life—I'd never known her to have a man, a pet, or a vice—was to study and write about Virginia Woolf. Though she taught drama, not English Lit, she had been working on a manuscript for almost ten years now. It was to be *the* critical work on Woolf, if it ever got finished and published.

"But I thought you were a full professor," I said. "How can they just sort of lay you off that way?"

"Full professor! Not by a long shot. No tenure, no stability."

We sat down amid the books. I felt awkward hiding the reason for my visit, so I just came out with it. I showed her the computer disk. "Do you have a printer . . . or a computer . . . or whatever . . . that can print this for me?"

She examined the disk for a second. "Oh, sure. The printer's in my study. I spend twelve hours a day in that damn room.... But first, tell me how you are."

Briefly, over a cup of dark tea, I told her about the savaging I had received for my role in *Beast in the Jungle*. Then I answered her questions, when I could, about the people we knew in common in New York. She seemed so lonely, hungry for news of any kind.

When I said I was staying for a few days at the Covington colony, Amanda looked puzzled. She made a slight face, as if she thought such a place was beneath me. It was an odd response; I'd never thought of Amanda as any kind of snob. But perhaps she disapproved of such places on some principle known only to herself. I didn't mention the Riverside String Quartet.

Then she asked if I was still interested in the Virginia Woolf project we had been discussing off and on for years. Amanda had begun work on a one-woman show based on Woolf's words, taken mainly from her diaries. I would be Virginia, of course. I said that I was still very much interested. She promised that one of these days she would finish it. And she reiterated that I would make a great V.W. "I'm tall enough, at any rate," I said, "and look good in long dresses."

"You have her neck, too, Alice. That's important. What about some more tea?"

"Well ..."

Amanda smiled at me. She knew I was impatient. She knew that whatever my reason, I wanted that disk printed now. She took it from my hand. I followed her into the study, where the imposing overflow of books from the other room threatened to take over here as well.

The "hard copy"—I don't know why they call paper that—was ready in minutes. "There was only a few pages' worth," she said as she handed them to me. "Wait!" She did a double take as she looked down at the first sheet. "Alice ... that name on the first page. Will Gryder. Alice, isn't he the one who was murdered the other day? My lord, when you told me where you were staying, I *thought* I recalled reading something about it in the paper! That's where it happened, isn't it?"

I nodded. Amanda released her hold on the short stack of papers. I stared down at the cover page, which read:

OUTLINE OF
UNSTRUNG
A novel by Will Gryder

The second sheet began:

When it comes to greed, backstabbing, and sexual promiscuity, the world of the classical music professional takes a backseat to no other entertainment milieu—not even rock 'n' roll.

I could hardly believe what I was reading. I began to giggle. And then I realized it wasn't funny. I read a little more:

This novel begins in New York in 1968. Four young women, two studying at Juilliard and two at the Mannes School, become friends.

I didn't need to read any more at the moment. I rolled up the sheets of paper. I had it! A big, fat, beautiful, seedy motive for murder. Will Gryder, pianist, composer, gourmet, and lothario, was about to become a trash novelist. He was writing a very thinly disguised "lives and loves" sort of thing about the Riverside Quartet. A pulp synthesis of Mary McCarthy's *The Group* and Kenneth Anger's *Hollywood Babylon*. But why shoot the piano player over that old tune? Sexual exposés are trivial nowadays. There had to be something else Will was going to write about. Something pretty bad. It had to be . . .

"What's going on, Alice?" Amanda demanded, obviously worried by the way my face was set.

I had a reason to get back to the house in Covington—John Cerise was going to call me. But that was many hours away, and I didn't want to be there if I didn't have to be. Beth Stimson had invited me up for a vacation. So I was out vacationing, enjoying myself for a change.

"Listen, Amanda. Do you have any of that project typed-up and handy?" I asked.

Her eyes grew wide with excitement. "Oh, yes! The first act, taken from the 1915 to 1919 diaries."

"May I take a look?"

"With pleasure."

For the next three hours I spoke Virginia Woolf's diaries, as edited by Amanda Avery. We even rigged up a stage set in her living room, using a piano bench and some knicknacks.

After the "performance" we drank strong coffee and talked about the possibilities for the script. It was fun. And it killed time. Later in the afternoon she made tuna sandwiches, which we had with some stale potato chips. It wasn't the kind of meal Mrs. Wallace was turning out back at the house, but it filled me up. I promised Amanda I'd be better about writing to her, and that I'd make an effort to get up to western Mass. more often.

I was back at Covington by six in the evening. I could hear laughter as I came in the front door.

Darcy, Mat Hazan, Roz, and Miranda were lounging around, but Ben Polikoff and Beth were nowhere in sight.

"I've got a new crop of viola jokes," Darcy said. "The last time I had lunch with Judy Nelson she told me a few good ones." She looked up and greeted me. "Come on in, Alice."

I said hello to the group, but stood tentatively near the door.

"How do you know when you have a viola section on your front porch? . . . You open the front door and none of them knows when to come in."

Roz appreciated that one.

"What's the difference between a violist and a lawn mower?"

"You can tune a lawn mower," Hazan answered. "That used to be a soprano joke."

The group, except for Miranda, began to be exceedingly polite to me, questioning me about my day. I told them I had visited friends in town and stopped at a few museums in the area, then I excused myself, saying that I needed to shower and change.

"Why are violists jokes so short?" I heard Darcy ask as I left. "So violinists can remember them."

Some tempting scents were wafting out of the kitchen. I heard Mrs. Wallace whistling as I climbed the stairs.

The phone rang at six minutes past seven. Beth yelled up the stairs that I had a call. I was already waiting by the telephone in the corridor. I picked up the receiver and waited till the downstairs extension had clicked off.

John had organized his information very well, and he relayed it to me efficiently and in sequence. I listened with growing awe and excitement, taking notes all the while. He spoke with virtually no interruption in the flow of the narrative for about twenty minutes, then stopped, asking, "Did I do all right, Miss Nestleton?"

"Beyond my wildest dreams, John."

"I bet," he said, "you say that to all the boys."

"Alice!"

I was so startled by the sound of someone calling my name that I instinctively thrust the notes I'd taken under my pillow. Beth was standing at the door to my room. "Aren't you coming to supper, Alice? Mrs. Wallace has outdone herself this time. I think she's cooked Amish—or do I mean Alsatian?"

"Thanks, but no, Beth. I'm not hungry."

"Well, then, come down for coffee and dessert.

"Mathew's going to play his pirated tapes of Callas in *Norma*."

"I won't miss *that*," I said.

A few minutes later I could hear them all at table. I went out to the hall and made a hurried call to Ford Donaldson. Nothing could happen without his help.

15

The room was warm as toast. And the musicians and their men were basking in the afterglow of the last chords in the immolation scene from something Teutonic.

I had a certain amount of interest in the murky Maria Callas tape—which, I learned, had been secretly recorded in Dallas—but the scary German selections that followed it made my skin crawl.

The music finally ended.

I had a midnight appointment with Ford Donaldson. I could barely wait.

Darcy was fiddling with a crossword puzzle, stopping every once in a while to relate another "lightbulb" joke that insulted violists. Mathew Hazan was scribbling in a spiral note pad. Beth was knitting leisurely with two lethal-looking needles, and the cat was skating around madly, snapping at the strings of purple yarn. Ben and Roz were dozing in facing armchairs, her feet in his lap. Miranda was stretched out on the sofa, entranced, it seemed, by whatever she was listening to on her Walkman. I was looking through a field guide to birds I'd found in the library, but my mind wasn't on it. I kept watching the clock and counting the *thuncks* Mrs. Wallace made on her board as she sat coring green apples at the dining room table.

At last, it was ten minutes to twelve.

I announced to the drowsy group: "I'm going out for a bit."

"What!" Beth looked at me in astonishment. "But it's freezing outside. And pitch-black! And besides, anybody could be . . . *waiting* out there."

Miranda sat up then. "Let her go, Beeswax," she said dismissively. "Can't you see the lady has a heavy date?"

"I'm sure I'm quite safe *outside*," I told Beth, ignoring Miranda. "I won't be gone long." I had a sudden desire to say that I was feeling a little "unstrung" and needed some air, using the title of Will Gryder's secret novel. But I suppressed the impulse.

I walked into the biting wind, plodding toward the road where I was to meet up with Donaldson. His car was there, the inside light on, motor idling. He reached over and wordlessly opened the door for me.

"I guess I've ruined your evening," I said apologetically, sliding in next to him.

"Part of the job description," he said stoically. "This couldn't wait till morning, right?"

"It couldn't, no. I know why Will Gryder was murdered."

He didn't say anything.

"And who killed him."

He didn't say anything.

I reached into my coat pocket and pulled out the four-page printout of *Unstrung.*

"What is this, Alice?"

"Read it."

He finished two of the four pages, then repeated, "What is this, Alice?"

"Exactly what it says it is!" His purposeful denseness was making me a little crazy. "A fictionalized treatment of the Riverside String Quartet and the people around them."

"Uh-huh." He brushed at some imaginary lint on his coat sleeve. "Are you telling me, Alice, that somebody murdered that man because he was about to tell who was sleeping with who?"

I took the pages back. "No, that isn't what he was going to tell—I mean, he was, but that was the least of it. He was going to reveal something much more serious than that."

"Like what?"

"Well . . . I can't tell you that right now."

I watched him slowly lower his head until it rested on the wheel. "Then why am I here?" he said weakly.

"To help me—that is, for me to help you—get the murderer—in the next twenty-four hours. Do you hear what I'm saying? You can clear the case by tomorrow night." I had used the term my policeman friend Rothwax always employed. Solving a murder was "clearing the case."

"Just tell me something," Ford said after a long minute. "Does this have anything to do with stuffed animals?"

"Really, Lieutenant! I want *you* to just tell *me* something: Do you want that murderer? Do you want to clear this case? In twenty-four hours?"

He was frightened to accept my offer. But obviously frightened not to.

"Listen, Alice, why can't you just tell me what

you know, and let me take your murderer in for questioning?"

"Because that won't work. Believe me. We've got to do this my way." Another uncomfortable silence followed, while Ford sat almost squirming with indecision.

"You really have nothing to lose, Ford," I said. "If I'm wrong, you'll be able to close the book on me, write me off as a fool. If I'm right, though . . ." I allowed him to fill in the blank.

He sighed. "All right. What do you want to do?"

"I have a trap all—" I began.

"One more question for you," he interrupted. "Just one more question. And I want you to answer it honestly."

"Go ahead."

"Have you recently been released from a mental facility of any kind?"

I pulled at the door handle, ready to leap from the car, but his hand on my arm stayed me.

"Okay, okay, okay. Settle down."

I managed to, but I wanted very badly to slap him.

"This isn't going to cost the state anything, is it? Because I'd have to have it authorized first."

"Not a penny," I said.

"Then I guess I'm your man."

I explained my plan to him, one step at a time. He listened very carefully, and seemed to understand everything.

And I still wanted to slap him.

16

"Alice, are you awake?"

Beth was peering into my room through the partially open door.

I pretended to be still dazed from sleep, though I'd been awake for an hour—waiting.

"What time is it?" I mumbled.

"About eight. Sorry if I woke you, but the officer just came to the door and said that Lieutenant Donaldson would be here in an hour. He's coming by with some information on the investigation, and he wants us all to be there."

"All right. I'll be down," I told her.

Good for Lieutenant Donaldson. He could be difficult, but when push came to shove he was indeed a good soldier. He was right on schedule, just as we had planned.

It was freezing in my room. The central-heating system had apparently given up the ghost in the wee hours of the morning. I was grateful that I was the last to get the use of the large bathroom I shared with Beth and Darcy. The heat and moisture from their morning showers still hung in the room. I finished bathing and went back to my room, shivering as I jumped into my clothes. I put on heavy slacks and a purple ribbed sweater, and on top of that a lined wool vest with very sweet cat appliqués on the pockets. Mrs. Oshrin, my New York neighbor, had made it for me one winter when we'd had boiler problems in the building.

I left the room and headed down the stairs. On the third step down, I suddenly stopped. Why was I so bloody cool? Was I so sure of my directorial abilities—sure that everything would go off as planned? And where did I get the confidence? I had bits and pieces of this case, that's all.

Little things send me around the bend, but in times of stress and danger I seem to become insufferably cool. I'm not a particularly brave woman. Is it arrogance? Right there on the steps, I had a piercing memory of a particular rehearsal of the play I'd been in—the role that had been panned. In the last scene I was on my deathbed. John Marcher, the tentative hero of *The Beast in the Jungle*, was at my side. I said to him that at least the fear which had always kept us apart would now be gone, after I was dead. He retorted that nothing would ever be in the past for him, until the day *he* dies. And that, he added, would be soon, because he couldn't survive my passing.

I was directed to reach out at that point and touch him gently on the face. As a sign of love, as a sign of loss, a sign of inexplicable tragedy. I said no. I told the director that I would keep my hands at my sides. I told him he did not understand May Bartram.

A burst of laughter from downstairs brought me out of my reverie. When I reached the bottom of the stairs I saw the source of the laughter—Mat Hazan. He was regaling those gathered with field mice stories. Mrs. Wallace was walking about, refilling coffee cups and offering brioches from a tray.

"Last night I was lying there in bed," Hazan went on, "and I heard this incredible racket. I looked up to see half a dozen mice stringing a banner across my window. I got up and put on my glasses. Sure enough, it was a banner. And on it were the words, 'They have Lake Placid. We have Covington Center.' I realized that I was a privileged man indeed. I would be the first to witness the field mouse winter Olympics. Some of the events are really quite special. Like bobsledding down the perilous milk bottle. Downhill skiing on wet socks. And the luge! It's performed on discarded ladybug shells. I even saw the opening ceremonies—and very moving they were, I'm here to tell you, what with that huge disposable lighter they were carrying around. And you'll never guess to whom the games were dedicated."

"Mickey Mouse," offered Darcy.

"Yo-Yo Ma," said Ben.

"Not even close," Mat said scornfully. Then he stood and pointed dramatically to the center of the room, where Lulu sat, lovely and unconcerned.

The laughter that followed terminated only when the doorbell rang and Ford Donaldson walked in.

"Good morning," he said solemnly. "Did I interrupt something?"

"Nothing that shouldn't have been interrupted," Beth said. "Just the ridicule of a helpless animal."

Ford took off his hat. He stood calmly in the

middle of the room, towering over the others like a stately oak. He was wearing a nice tie, a rather daring one in fact, considering his mono-chromatic tastes.

"I won't take up too much of your time," he said. "I just wanted to bring you up to date on the status of things." That was good, I thought: spoken rather humbly, but not groveling or out of character.

"The investigation is proceeding," he contin-ued. "Maybe not as fast as any of us would like. But we are still on it full-time. To date, we haven't recovered anything taken from Mr. Gryder—credit cards, jewelry, what have you. We continue to believe that the murder occurred during a robbery, and the likely suspect is either a local or one of the many drifters who pass through this neck of the woods. I know that's not very much, but we've got our eyes and ears open and sooner or later there'll be a break."

Beautiful! I thought. Ford Donaldson was a better actor than many a professional I'd worked with.

Our eyes met ever so briefly as he looked around the room, waiting for questions, com-ments.

But there were none. The old sadness was back on the faces of every member of the group, and I saw Ben clench his jaw, as if willing him-self not to voice his complaint about the lack of progress in the case.

Ford's face was grave, too. "I also thought you'd want to know that the coroner has re-leased the body," he announced. "It's being— Mr. Gryder's remains are being shipped to his sister in California." He paused here, nodded good day to us, and turned toward the door.

Now, I silently instructed him. *Now, Ford, turn back to the audience.* The Good Soldier followed my orders.

He took a few steps back into the room. "There's one favor I would ask of you. We found a white canvas duffel bag belonging to Gryder. It had been hidden in one of the old stone wells on the property. Any of you folks know of a reason for that?"

I could feel the tension rise suddenly in the audience. No one answered Donaldson's question, but they were all murmuring, looking nervously at one another.

"No . . . ?" Ford said. "Well, we can't figure out why he would have put it there. But in any case, the lab's finished with it. It contained nothing of interest to us—some papers and computer supplies. We stowed it in one of the sheds by the creek, the larger one, and I'm sending an officer around for it tomorrow. I figured we'd ship it off to Mr. Gryder's sister at the same time as the body. Would one of you be good enough to point the shed out to my men when he gets here?"

"Of course," Mat Hazan said.

"We'll even give him a cup of tea," Darcy offered. "Won't we, Mrs. Wallace?" But the cook had vanished into her kitchen.

Ford waved his thanks and was through the door. I exhaled. Bravo, Donaldson! Economy of words. Economy of motion. A great performance, even as he pulled open the teeth of the trap.

"Can you believe what he said about Will

burying a duffel bag in the well?" Roz asked as soon as the door had swung shut.

"I didn't even know there *was* a well," Darcy remarked.

"The locals don't tell you," said Miranda. "Primarily because they hope you'll fall in."

I didn't participate in the conversation. I walked to the space between the dining room and the kitchen and called out strongly to the cook: "Mrs. Wallace, I won't be here for dinner this evening. I'm seeing a friend this afternoon, and will probably be spending the night at his place."

"Bragging, Alice?" Beth asked naughtily.

I had spoken loudly enough for all to hear. It was necessary to establish a plausible explanation for my absence.

For a minute, I didn't know whether Mrs. Wallace had heard me. But presently she grunted her understanding.

I helped myself to the coffee that had been left on the dining room table. It was still reasonably hot. I blew on it a little over the rim of my cup, and my eye caught Lulu stretching and yawning on top of the china cabinet. She seemed very relaxed, very pleased with her new life.

I felt good, too. Donaldson and I, so far, were a wonderful team. I just hoped it would not turn out to be a vaudeville act.

17

"I hope you appreciate how ridiculous I feel here, Alice."

I smiled in the darkness. At long last, I was getting the chance to patronize *him* a little.

It was seven P.M. We were, all things considered, comfortable in our hiding place behind a pile of cartons in the shed. Across the aisle, on the same blanket where Beth and Will had made love, was a white canvas duffel. I had stuffed it with all manner of junk and twisted the drawstrings around a six-dollar padlock, so that to open the strings one had either to undo the lock or cut the strings.

We were each seated on a carton covered with a blanket, behind two larger boxes that prevented anyone coming down the narrow aisle from spotting us. We had removed the single overhead bulb at the entrance. The darkness was severe.

I finally responded to his remark. "Why should you feel foolish? Police work is about surveillance, isn't it? Just hang in there, Ford."

A few minutes later I heard a crinkling sound. A ripple went up my spine. In setting up this stakeout, I had never given a thought—until now—to rats! But then I realized the sound was being made by Donaldson. "What *is* that?" I snapped.

"LifeSaver. Want one?"

"Thank you, no."

He let a few more minutes go by.

"Are you married, Alice?"

"Not for some time now."

"Neither am I," he said.

"Yes. I thought as much. . . . Let me tell you again how sorry I am about monopolizing your evenings lately."

I heard him sigh.

I'd spent enough time with the man to make a few educated guesses about the source of his temper, his burden. It seemed fairly clear he was no secret drinker, and neither a disgruntled employee nor a cocaine addict. Love problems, I had decided. An affair. That was the cause of his trouble.

"Think we're in for a long haul, do you?" he asked, with just a touch of amusement in his voice.

"More than likely," I said, matching his tone. "Just hang in there."

He took another candy. "So you're an actress."

"When I'm working."

"Ever in the movies?"

"No, never. I did some TV work years ago. But mostly the stage."

"I get down to New York every once in a blue moon," he said.

"Oh, really?" I didn't know what was coming next. I thought he might be about to invite me out to dinner on his next visit. Or perhaps call me to task—as a lot of people I meet do—for all the crime, dirt, and unhappiness in New York.

"Yes," said Ford. "I've got a sister living in New York. She went down there twenty-five years ago to study music. Wanted to be an opera singer. But it didn't work out."

"It usually doesn't," I said sympathetically.

"Last time I was down there, I saw a play."

"Good for you."

"Yeah, it was a privilege."

"What was a privilege?"

"Mr. Eugene O'Neill," he announced. "*A Moon for the Misbegotten*. Had to go out there to Brooklyn, but that was okay. Ever see it?"

"No," I lied. I wasn't about to get into what I thought of O'Neill. Just seeing this new aspect of the enigmatic Lieutenant Donaldson was enough for me.

It was about ten-thirty when he asked me, "Any predictions about what time this killer's going to show up?"

"I would think some time after eleven," I said. "Those dinners can run a little late, depending on what Mrs. Wallace cooks up. And then there's dessert . . . and coffee . . . and brandy . . . and . . ."

"Might be a while, eh?"

"Yes, Ford."

"Or never?"

"Or never," I repeated. "Anything's possible."

I heard him blowing into his hands against the cold. Then, just when I was wondering if he was too macho to wear gloves, he plucked a pair out of the pocket of his jacket.

"All this for a lousy diskette," he mumbled.

"It's what the murderer thinks is on that diskette, Lieutenant. And then, there is something else."

"Something else? You didn't tell me about anything else."

"No. But I'm going to tell you now. The killer is also after some papers, papers that lay out cat pedigrees. That's what this whole thing is about."

Nothing. A yawning silence. I knew that he was trying to get himself under control before speaking.

He said, finally, "Let's just agree to something—okay? You won't explain what you just said until we have the killer in custody—okay? Because I just don't want to hear about it now. Deal?"

"Yes, Ford."

I could suddenly feel the cold in every part of my body. I wanted to move, but couldn't. And I could sense Donaldson's slightest gesture in the darkness, as though every movement were a potential threat to me. I kept my eyes on the luminous dial of his wristwatch, watching the minutes roll slowly by.

My stomach began to turn cartwheels. At last I stood up and walked in tiny circles. I heard Donaldson say something. I thought he chuckled evilly, too.

"What was that you said?"

"I said, you really hate them, don't you?"

"Who?"

"Those musician friends of yours."

"What makes you think that?"

"I watched you with them. It's obvious."

We had both fallen to whispering, engaging in a kind of desperate, pregnant dialogue.

"It is no such thing, Ford. Beth and Roz and the others are great musicians," I said.

"Yeah? So why do you hate them?"

"Please stop this."

"All right. If you won't tell me why you hate them, then tell me why you're so cool and calm now. If you're not an escapee from the booby hatch, we ought to have a killer walking in here soon. He might even try to kill *you*. Why are you so calm?"

Before I could answer, a thump somewhere silenced me. Ford and I froze where we were, waiting for the shed door to swing open. But it didn't.

"Probably a raccoon," he said after five minutes. "Be a shame if I had to shoot him. But if he isn't carrying his pedigree papers, shoot him I will. That's just the way it is up here."

Donaldson's glow-in-the-dark watch showed eleven forty-five.

I dozed off a little. Bushy and Pancho and Basillio and my favorite quilt and my favorite bakery and all the other familiar things in life danced around on the edge of my consciousness.

"Quarter past one, Alice."

I snapped awake.

"Looks like your killer is a little behind schedule."

"No, she's not!" I said, and grabbed Ford's wrist in a silencing gesture.

The clang against the shed door felt electric, as if my foot had touched the third rail on the IRT. I sensed Donaldson moving for his gun.

The door opened, and a gust of freezing air

coursed through the shed. Then the door closed easily. The killer was here with us!

A flashlight beam traveled down the aisle. And then the footsteps began, moving tentatively, the killer looking, looking for the white duffel.

I pressed back tight against the carton, my hands folded, turning white. Ford brushed against me as he inched forward silently.

I saw a figure. Directly in front of us, in the aisle, facing the duffel. The figure bent over and began to pull at the bag. I heard an intake of breath. I heard hands struggling to open the bag, and then the short break in breathing when the killer realized it was padlocked.

Then Donaldson tapped my shoulder to signal me, and I flicked on his powerful highway-cop flashlight, bathing the startled figure in its beam.

"Can I help you?" Donaldson said quietly, almost wryly, but the words reverberated with menace. Only then did I see the weapon in his hand, held straight out.

"Drop that flashlight!" he ordered. "Don't turn around! Raise your arms over your head!"

The plastic torch fell to the floor with a clang.

"Now turn around slowly."

When Miranda Bly turned to face us, her eyes nearly rolled up into her head. She was dressed preposterously: a sweatshirt and a thermal nylon vest, worn over a nightgown with a Peter Rabbit print. She had on a Russian-style mink hat.

"Miss Bly, isn't it?" Ford said. "Please explain what you're doing here."

She looked dumbly from Ford's face to mine.

Her own face seemed absurdly elongated in the horror-white glare of the flashlight.

"Let me explain, Lieutenant," I said, moving in. "Miss Bly is looking for some papers discussing the lineage of a particular breed of cat. And for a computer diskette with the beginning of a book Will Gryder was writing. Miss Bly had to stop that book's being written—at any cost. Isn't that so, Miranda?"

She still did not speak.

So I continued. "The Riverside String Quartet did not get its start through the financial benevolence of Roz Polikoff's Aunt Sarah—if indeed there ever was such a person. No, they raised the necessary capital by more shocking means. Miranda and Roz are the only ones who know that the Aunt Sarah story is a lie. It was the two of them who provided the money. And they got it by stealing litters of Scottish Fold kittens, back when they were young women working in an expensive pet store in New York. The kittens were commanding seven hundred dollars apiece back then, in the mid-seventies, even though the breed hadn't even been officially recognized. The kittens were just adorable—and people with the money wanted them. Then, something much worse than theft happened. Didn't it, Miranda?"

She didn't answer me, but stared down at the flashlight she had dropped to the floor. Its beam was still shining on my boots.

Lieutenant Donaldson gestured for me to go on.

"A man looking after the grounds where some of the cats were bred was shot one night when he stumbled upon a theft in progress. He pulled through, but he was paralyzed for life. No one was ever charged with the crime. But somehow Will Gryder found out about Roz and Miranda's involvement. And somehow Miranda found out that Will knew. Miranda may not have known what kind of book it was, but she thought Will was going to tell the whole story of what had happened, naming her and Roz. And she knew she had to stop him. Maybe she tried to bribe him. Maybe she thought sleeping with him would change his mind. But she failed. And one night, she killed him. It was Miranda who drove that chisel into his heart, and believe me, Lieutenant Donaldson, a woman who has been playing the cello all those years has the strength in her shoulders and arms to do it."

I realized I was talking too fast, but I couldn't seem to slow down. The two of them seemed to be crowding me. I started to move around as I talked.

"I don't think it was premeditated. I just think she slipped out of the main house at a time when no one would notice, found Will in the barn and begged him, cajoled him, threatened him—whatever—and then when it didn't work, killed him in a fury. Once she realized what she'd done, she wiped off the weapon, took his money and other effects, and disposed of them somewhere, to make it seem like a robbery. Then she went back and joined the others. I don't know how, but the next day she caused that accident. It was some sort of warning to Roz—or maybe Miranda really did hope Roz would die—because she realized it could only have been Roz who'd told Will about the Scottish Fold cats, when he and Roz were lovers."

I had finished my runaway analysis.

Donaldson blew out a long breath. "You've been a busy girl, Alice. I assume all that stuff about the cats and the assault on the watchman will check out?"

"It comes from an impeccable source."

"Go and put the light back in, will you?" he asked me.

It was not until I'd done as Ford had asked that Miranda spoke. "Are you quite finished?" she said. "Both of you?"

I answered. "Yes, Miranda. Why?"

She shook her head slowly, then began to laugh derisively. "You should absolutely be under lock and key. You're a public menace, you crazy bitch. And as for you, Lieutenant Donaldson, words fail me at the moment. But I hope that won't be true when it comes time for your hearing before the police review board. You're both insane—the both of you."

Ford said nothing.

"Look," she said impatiently to him, "put your hand in my pocket—go ahead. I'd do it myself, if I didn't think you'd blow my brains out."

He reached into her vest pocket and extracted what looked for all the world like a string of real pearls.

"Yes, that's right," she said disgustedly. "Look at it, you ass! It's a pearl necklace, I wanted to send it to Will's sister Carolyn. She and I had been best friends since we were ten years old. When we were in school Willy said he couldn't afford to buy two necklaces, so he gave this to us to share—because we were so close. And we did. Except we had a horrible falling out more than fifteen years ago. We never spoke again.

I've been in my room crying about it—about this whole horrible thing—all night, and I thought I could just come out here and put it into that bag with his things. She would know what it meant."

Ford looked at me.

"As for the obscene charge that I murdered Willy," Miranda said, almost screaming now, "this ridiculous woman has been trying to get something on us all from the minute she walked into our lives! But I didn't kill him! How could I? At the time they say he died, I was in Mat's room making love with him."

The moment she spoke those words, Ford's confidence in me collapsed. I knew it. And Miranda knew it.

"Why don't I just give this necklace to you, Lieutenant," she said. "You and your state troopers or whatever the hell you are can unlock that thing and ... insert it—and you know where."

The three of us walked in silence through the freezing night. Ford did not look at me once, but our two flashlights kept crisscrossing on the ground.

As soon as we were inside the house, Miranda wheeled on Donaldson, speaking through clenched teeth. "Let's get this over with right now, shall we? I want you to confirm what I said this instant. Talk to Mat."

By the time we were halfway up the stairs the whole house was up, wondering who was making the commotion at two in the morning. Miranda told them.

She told them in the most graphically scatalogical terms I'd ever heard used by an educated woman from a good home. And she ended the diatribe by saying it was all Beth's fault for having asked me here.

I turned my back on the look Beth Stimson gave me. I stood watching Ford accompany Mathew Hazan into his room to speak with him alone. Now being calmed and comforted by the circle of her comrades, one of the nicer things Miranda called me was a "fiend." Ford was out of Mat's room in less than fifteen minutes. He finally looked at me, and it was with sadness rather than rage.

I went into my second-class citizen's room and was packed in ten minutes. I looked around for Lulu, but I couldn't find her. I wanted to say good-bye.

Ford walked with me to my car.

"Win a few, lose a few, Alice," Ford said as I turned the motor over.

I had no trouble finding the road back to New York.

18

I was trying to convince Bushy I was happy to see him. But I don't think he believed me—probably because I was crying my eyes out.

As soon as I entered my apartment I fell onto the sofa and began to weep. But at the same time I was trying to embrace the befuddled Bushy. He backed away stiffly, his eyes never leaving my face. I knew I'd be paying for abandoning the cats for some time to come. Pancho wasn't around, but I could hear him scrabbling around on the high cabinets in the kitchen.

I could see that Tony had piled the mail and messages on the long dining room table. He had obviously made an effort to be neat, but the piles had collapsed and mail was scattered everywhere.

His carefully built hill of letters had probably collapsed as quickly and thoroughly as my murder case had—as easily as Miranda Bly had punctured it.

Not only had my trap proved futile, even ludicrous, but I had literally been thrown off the premises. Yes, I'd been shown to be less than a stellar crime solver. But my tears were also for the shame I felt—the humiliation. Start to finish I'd been patronized, tolerated, ignored, talked down to by that group of self-important musicians. They'd made me feel like an unwanted child. And why? Because *I* didn't have any inside dirt on Lenny Bernstein. *I* didn't go to cocktail parties with Jamie Laredo, or own any bootleg cassettes of Maria Callas. For the Riverside String Quartet, that was enough of a reason.

Of course, I knew now the nature of my mistake. I realized now why everything had gone wrong. It had all been based on a pivotal mistake: I had not understood that Mat Hazan was part of the original cat-theft ring; probably, in fact, the ringleader. And because I had left him out of the equation, it never dawned on me that they would cook up such a simple but persuasive alibi—that he and Miranda were making love in the house while Will Gryder was being murdered.

I knew in my bones I was right—knew what had transpired. I *had* shaped all the information John Cerise had fed me into a coherent explanation. But it was all ashes now—all of it. I'd never work for Beth Stimson again. She hated me now. The six of them had all come together in the face of my threat. But that is, I suppose, what a united group of any kind is all about, precisely what the critics had flayed the Riverside Quartet alive for failing to do: playing together, sticking together, acting as one.

Bushy was slowly moving toward me again, obliquely, as if on tiptoe. Pancho stuck his head into the living room for a minute. "Oh, so you've come crawling back to us," is what he seemed to be saying. "So what?" And off he ran on his perpetual rounds.

There's a lot I should do, I told myself: Call

Basillio to let him know I've come back early; go over and thank Mrs. Oshrin for all her help; call my agent and various cat-sitting clients. I blew my nose and picked up a yellow pad and pencil. It was only then that Bushy deigned to join me on the couch. He liked to chew erasers.

Sitting there with pad and pencil in hand, the thought came to me that I ought to write Ford Donaldson. But what was I going to say to him? Sorry I couldn't produce your murderer as promised? But I believed I had. Sorry you had to camp out for seven freezing hours in a dilapidated shed? Sorry I wasn't quick enough to understand all the ramifications of the conspiracy?

No, I wasn't going to write any of that. It was best to leave it alone.

I was punch-drunk with exhaustion. After all, I'd been up all night, had driven nonstop all the early morning. I fell fast asleep in the middle of scratching Bushy's ruff.

"What is going *on* here, Swede?"

I was looking into Tony Basillio's grinning face.

"Listen, madam, I was hired to feed two cats and two cats only. I come here in good faith to do my job, and look what I find. Well, I'm sorry, Swede, but my contract is quite clear—*two* cats."

Still groggy, I felt Tony kissing the top of my head. Then he helped me to a sitting position and placed a cup of black coffee in my hand and stepped back.

"What time is it, Basillio?"

"One in the afternoon. Are you home to stay, or just grabbing a change of thermal underwear?"

"Oh, I'm back. Am I ever. I've been run out of the state of Massachusetts."

I drank from the coffee cup. My head and body ached dully. I needed a bath in the worst way. And I was starving.

I handed the cup back when I was finished. "What's your financial situation, Tony?"

"Relatively flush—hundred and thirty-five bucks, cash."

"Know what I want? I want a glass of red wine and the biggest, bloodiest hamburger in town—with tomato and onion . . . and no bun."

"It's yours. I plight thee my troth. Let us away."

"After my bath," I said. "Can you feed the cats for me?"

Less than an hour later we were sitting in a booth in a serviceable bar and grill on Second Avenue. I was taking lusty gulps of my red wine and waiting for the burger to arrive.

"Boy, do you look unhappy," Tony said.

"Well, I am."

"Why don't you tell Uncle Tony what happened up there?"

I guess I needed to do just that. I narrated the train of events that had transpired from the moment I'd picked up the car and joined the queue on the Taconic Parkway, all the way up to sobbing on my sofa this morning. In fact I got so caught up in my own story that when I'd finished it, my food—which had been delivered during the scene where Mrs. Wallace was force-feeding me English muffins—was now cold. I picked along the edges of the hamburger.

Tony was looking at me strangely. "Something bothering you, Basillio?" I said.

"Well, not exactly 'bothering.' But ... well, I was just thinking ... isn't it possible that Miranda really *was* just feeling guilty about her friend and wanted to send that necklace to her?"

"Anything's possible, Tony—theoretically."

"What I mean to say is, no offense, but your whole trip up there seems so farfetched."

"Farfetched? What an interesting word choice. What, precisely, do you find so farfetched?'

"To be honest, everything ... the whole *schmeer*. Stolen Scottish cats. The novel. Aunt Bessie, or whatever her name was supposed to be—who doesn't really exist. The whole milieu, shall we say, is very unbelievable."

"What are you saying, Tony? That nothing I described to you really happened? That it didn't exist in the real world?"

"No, of course not. I just—"

"Look, don't try to ... evaluate it ... like someone trying to be *truthful* onstage. Or like a stage *set*, in your present case. It wasn't a piece frozen in time."

"Okay. I'm just saying it's hard to believe this Riverside Quartet—this group of serious, highly trained musicians, for godsake—is so collectively wicked. No, 'wicked' is not the word. I mean 'conspiratorial.' The way you tell it, it's like you were thrown in among a pride of lionesses who were perpetually in some kind of feeding frenzy."

I pushed my plate away, having eaten the sodden, pale tomato. Tony's imagery struck some kind of chord. At first I hadn't thought of the quartet and the men around them as raging lions, because what was between them was hidden, internecine. It was only after one spent time with them all, only after one became, for whatever reason, open to them, that one sensed their collectively predatory nature. And that was probably why the whole episode had so exhausted and defeated me.

"Hey, listen, Swede," he said, pushing back his long black hair with both hands, "you can't win em all. What's so funny?"

"Nothing. It's just that Ford Donaldson tried a very similar cliché on me. 'Win a few, lose a few' was the one he chose. Now you're telling me I can't win them all."

"Why do you think they call them clichés? They're common expressions."

"Hmm. Spoken with uncommon valor," I noted, not really knowing what I meant by that. Goodness, I *was* tired, when one glass of mediocre California red could make me so foolish. I ordered another.

"Should have taken me up there with you," Tony said.

"Why?"

"Because I have a tin ear. I'd have been more objective."

That was hilarious, I thought.

Well, in any case, it was good to be home.

19

I have always liked that expression, "getting back in the swing of things." It's hard to say what it really means, but one always knows whether or not one has accomplished it.

It took about a week after my return from the Covington Art Center for the rhythm of my life to regain anything remotely resembling "swing."

It was two weeks before I managed to stop poring over what I had found in Will Gryder's room—the old photographs, the faded cat breeding charts, the little computer disk—examining the items, over and over, in a kind of bewildered nostalgia. Had I really been all wrong about the case? Was my version of the facts "farfetched"? And what was I supposed to do with the things now—send them to Will's sister?

By the end of week three, the memory of the Riverside String Quartet was like the memory of a toothache. I stopped talking about them, stopped worrying about them, and thought about them only to be thankful that the dull, throbbing pain of it all was gone.

Tony, however, had become obsessed with one element of it, and one element only: Lulu's failure to chase the mice. For the hundredth time he asked me, "Why wouldn't she go after the mice, Swede? Didn't you ever figure out why not?"

No, I had to say again. I never did.

He said maybe the dog was blind, maybe she had lost her sense of smell. I reminded him that Lulu was a cat, not a dog. He replied that he knew that; he just liked that old country saying so much—"That dog won't hunt"—that he used it for cats and people and elephants. In fact, the mystery of why Lulu wouldn't hunt began to derange poor Basillio. He started demanding that I let him move in; he moaned that he was weary of occasional sex and occasional intimacy; said that my intermittent coldness toward him was the real reason his return to the world of stage design had been such a spectacular failure—even for him, a man who cultivated failure with a passion.

Tony's incomprehensible flights were only part and parcel of getting back into the swing of things.

And then the swing broke, about a week before Thanksgiving.

My phone rang that cold Tuesday morning. I picked up, and was startled to hear the voice at the other end of the line.

"Alice, hello! This is Leo Trilby."

Why was the director of the *Beast in the Jungle* fiasco phoning me? We were by no means friends. We hadn't even gotten along as co-workers—not during rehearsals and not during the run—if those few pitiful performances could be called a "run."

"Look, Alice, I'm going to be in your neighborhood this afternoon. You know that Italian place on Twenty-ninth and Third? Why don't we meet there—about three. I thought I could buy you a cappuccino."

I didn't answer.

"You like cappuccino, don't you? And cheese-cake?"

It was hard to know what to say. I liked them very much.

"I thought perhaps I ought to mend some fences," Leo said by way of greeting. He was waiting for me at one of the small round tables, tense and hyperactive as ever. Leo Trilby was barely out of his twenties, actually, but he had an affected British air that made him seem much older. No doubt he'd picked up his mannerisms during his studies at Oxford. He *was* rather brilliant, though, his mind constantly racing with theories and leaping ahead so fast that his directorial instructions were incomprehensible.

He began to talk as soon as I sat down. "It wasn't your fault, you know, and it wasn't my fault, either. One simply shouldn't try to modernize Henry James. But that was the playwright's mistake, wasn't it? I mean, God! He, James, that is, was modern enough for his age. But you can't turn his insights into wisdom for the nineties, can you? Are you with me on that, Alice?"

"Oh, I don't know, Leo."

He leaned in toward me. He was a short, powerfully built man and he was wearing a turtleneck, which only enhanced the physical resemblance to the young Norman Mailer. His face was blunt. He had thick black hair, badly shorn, and thick eyebrows, and his constantly roving eyes were deep in their sockets.

"It is so terribly hard for people like us in this business, isn't it?" he said.

"It surely is, Leo," I said, savoring the not-too-sweet cheesecake that was the specialty of the café.

"I mean, one would be hard pressed to name a better actress in your age category, Alice. And where has it gotten you? Are you Streep? Are you Close? Are you even Cher? No. And you never will be, my dear. As for me, I'm good—damn good. We both know that. But I can never connect with the money. The money, the money, the money! The money people will always look upon me as an *enfant terrible*, when really I'm not that at all. I simply have my principles."

Leo sat back and exhaled hugely. He lit a cigarette and then stubbed it out immediately.

"If I gave you a hard time, Alice, forgive me. I want to be your friend. I want to be your colleague. And mark my words, the wheel will turn again. We *will* be together again someday—I know it. The wheel simply has to turn in our direction sometime. In our business, Alice, something always happens."

I had little idea what he was talking about. But I nodded in complete agreement, picking up crumbs of pie crust with my fork.

"Yes, the wheel always turns," he repeated. And then, as if to buttress his position, he picked up his folded *New York Times* and waved it under my nose. "Did you see this stunning piece of news? They're about to spend *six million* dollars on that lame-brained musical from England." Leo thrust the newspaper at me. It was turned to the entertainment section.

I read only a few sentences of the article about

the impending arrival of a splashy new musical based on a Jane Austen novel. I stopped reading it because I caught sight of the boldface heading over another, much shorter article: RIVERSIDE STRING QUARTET WILL DISBAND, the title read.

The story was simple. The Riverside String Quartet, the first and most celebrated all-woman chamber music group, had announced that after nearly twenty years it was disbanding as a result of personal difficulties and professional differences among its members. The article went on to detail the history of the group, its most successful tours and recordings, and the critical acclaim the women had enjoyed over the years.

The last paragraph of the article announced that Mathew Hazan, the longtime business manager/agent of the quartet, would soon take up a high administrative position at the prestigious John F. Kennedy Center in Washington, D.C.

I continued to stare down at the type on the page, dazed. Leo's mouth continued to move. I didn't hear a word.

How could this have happened? I knew that the group was up at Covington on a retreat because their European performances had been so poorly received. I knew that the death of Will Gryder had hurt them both as a group and individually. But to dismantle the quartet after all these years? It didn't make sense ... unless ... unless my failed trap had put the fear of God into at least two of the members. Unless they were terribly frightened by what Miranda Bly must have told them after I'd left.

But this had to be Hazan's doing. He was the beast in that jungle. And not only had he escaped scot-free, he was also dissolving the quartet and was about to start a wildly lucrative and coveted job. The man should be in a sewer somewhere.

Leo kept talking. I could hear him again. He was telling me he had to leave now, but he'd be seeing me again soon, working with me—the very thought of it nourished and excited him, he said.

And then he was gone, and I was alone at the table. He had carried the *Times* away with him. My rage was growing, suffocating me. It was like being zippered into a tight dress. I would *not* allow Mat Hazan to get away with this! I could not sit by and watch him move on, like a slick record-company entrepreneur, from one label to another. Not when he was leaving a trail of murder and deceit behind him.

I decided to clear this case, at whatever cost.

The waiter was a nice young man they called Lucky. He set another cappuccino down in front of me. There would be no charge for it, I knew. But I was too angry to drink it.

20

"What time is it, Bushy?"

The cat didn't answer me, so I pulled his tail gently. He *hates* that.

"Ha ha," I said, and kissed him on the nose. I stood up to go after another cup of coffee.

"Why the hell are you asking your cat for the time?" Tony yelled into the kitchen. "Does he own a watch? Huh? It's ten P.M. Do you know where your other cat is?"

I took my usual seat on the rug, next to Bushy. Arrayed at my feet were the items I'd brought back from Covington: the disk, the photos, the pedigree papers, Will's notes for his roman à clef. In my mind the items had by now taken on a kind of totemic quality.

"Here's how I figure your meeting with Leo," Tony said knowingly. "He's heard that you're being considered for something big-time. And he wants in. It's not another off-off-and-under-Broadway thing. I mean a big-ticket deal."

I merely nodded. I had no idea whether Tony's speculations were worth anything. But whatever Leo Trilby was up to, it didn't interest me in the least.

Tony came over and stared down at the objects on the floor. "Isn't that against the law, by the way? You stole evidence in a murder case."

"Wrong!" I snapped. "For one, I *found* the evidence, I didn't steal it. And two, Donaldson doesn't believe it has any meaning. He doesn't even consider it evidence. So at least as long as I have it, they're still frightened."

"Oh, yeah. They're shaking in their booties."

"Don't be so quick to scoff. I promise you, Mathew Hazan will soon be shaking in his. I'm going to get him!"

"Why don't you give it a rest, girl? What's it to you if the Riverside Quartet breaks up? Where's all this self-righteous ire coming from?"

"I'm not being self-righteous, Basillio. I just happen to take the concept of justice very seriously."

"Whoa! Aren't we getting a little messianic here?"

"Basillio, *you* didn't see that chisel in Will's chest. And all that awful blood. I did."

"I know that. But first it's the breakup of the group that makes you mad. Then it's the hateful manager. Now it's the horrible memory of finding the body—and the idea that justice has been cheated. Your motivations are all over the map, Miss Nestleton. You're way out of focus!"

"Am I? Well, watch me get back into character!" I snarled as I headed for the telephone.

"What are you doing?"

"Calling Beth Stimson," I said.

"Why?"

"Because I've got to make her listen to me. I've got to explain why I did what I did. And ask her help in continuing the investigation. To persuade her that Mathew Hazan and his henchman Miranda are murderers."

I half expected the answering machine to click on. But it was Beth herself who answered.

"Beth, this is Alice Nestle—"

The receiver was slammed down ferociously.

"Bad connection?" Tony asked disingenuously.

"She hung up on me." I dialed the number again. As soon as she picked up I began speaking desperately: "Please, Beth, let me—" But the phone clicked off again. It was no use.

"One thing I've always said about you, Swede. You've got the knack for making friends wherever you go."

"If all you can do is make wisecracks, Tony, why don't you just leave?"

He threw up his arms. "I've got a better idea," he said in resignation. "Why don't I make some pasta?"

I wasn't paying much attention to him. My mind was on other things.

"How would that be, Swede? Hungry?"

"Whatever," I mumbled. He disappeared into the kitchen, Bushy trailing along behind him.

It was obvious Beth Stimson wasn't going to listen to me. What next? How to restart a stone-cold investigation? I thought of a move: Call John Cerise again. He had given me solid information on the Scottish Fold thefts back in the 1970s. Maybe there was more where that came from. Maybe John knew more, or knew others who did.

I called him and, in a refreshing change of pace, *he* seemed delighted to hear my voice.

"Did what I gave you help any?" he asked.

"A great deal, John—but I need more."

He laughed softly. "Alice, sometimes I think you're part cat. You always want more."

"I know I'm being awfully pushy. And I'll make it up to you soon. But I need to contact the people whose litters were stolen. Or anyone who was involved on some basic level: vets, buyers, breeders. Anyone. I need names and addresses and phone numbers, John."

There was a lengthy pause, and I heard him take a deep breath. I wondered if there was someone there with him in the house.

"John, dear, am I calling at a bad time? I guess this could wait till morning."

"No, no. It isn't that. I was just taken aback. You know, that information I got for you . . . Well, you have to remember, those things happened twenty years ago, Alice. I have no idea where all those people are today, if indeed they're all still alive. But I guess I could give it a try, if you can give me a few days to work on it. Okay? I'll see what I can come up with."

"Thank you, John, thank you very much." We made a little small talk and then said good-bye.

I began to pace. I had little confidence in John's ability to come up with those names and numbers, in view of what he'd said. And I had no time! While I was up in New England I'd had no sense of "Time's wingèd chariot," but from the moment I saw that article in the *Times* about the dissolution of the Riverside and Hazan's new assignment, all I'd been able to think of was time passing. This had to be done quickly— *now*—or not at all.

All I really had were the cat thefts in the seventies. I had to concentrate on those. There had to be some kind of trail that could be followed. There had to be some source of information other than John Cerise.

I kept pacing. First Bushy came in to watch me. And then Tony.

"You ought to put on a pair of sneakers if you're going to keep this up." Tony was holding a couple of unpeeled garlic cloves.

"I haven't even *started* pacing yet, Tony. When I really get going I take in the hallway and the bedroom too."

"Well, it's always good to expand your horizons."

It was a mildly funny line, but I didn't laugh. I didn't laugh because his comment opened up a possibility for me. What if Miranda and Roz had expanded *their* horizons? What if their kitten-napping ring was in fact a large-scale organization that operated even outside the local area?

And maybe their thefts had stopped not because they'd reached a financial goal but because they'd been caught—or at least suspected by the authorities. In fact, if they stole one type of property, why not other types? Perhaps one or both of them had even been arrested in the past.

If any of that was true, there would be a record somewhere.

"Who are you calling now?"

"Remember Detective Rothwax? My old colleague from the police?"

"I remember him well," Tony said balefully, and headed back into the kitchen.

Rothwax didn't sound overjoyed to hear my voice. But luckily, I knew his bark was a great deal worse than his bite.

"Well, I'll be damned," he said. "It's Cat Woman. You keeping yourself out of trouble?"

When he'd first called me by that name, while I was a short-lived consultant for the NYPD special unit called RETRO, it had infuriated me. He seemed to have a talent for infuriating me back then. But we had eventually become good friends and he had helped me out often.

"Detective Rothwax, I need that darling little computer of yours again."

"So what else is new?" he said. "I didn't think you were calling to find out how my goldfish are doing."

"Seriously, can you help?"

"Who do you want checked out this time?"

"Four women."

"What kinds of dirt are we looking for?"

"Arrest records. Any kind of contact with the law. Any kind of anything, I guess."

"Who are they?"

"Musicians."

"You don't say."

"Yes, I do. Classical musicians who belong to a rather famous chamber music group."

"Nobody like you, Cat Lady. Nobody."

I spelled all their names for him and gave him the few trivial bits of hard information I had on each. Naturally, it didn't go much farther than knowing that Beth Stimson was from Denver, or that Roz was married to a well-to-do businessman.

"Do you think you can have something for me tomorrow?" I asked. "I could meet you at RETRO." I hoped that my voice echoed my sense of urgency.

"Sure. Why not? If they put the cuffs on me

for unauthorized use of the computer, you can accompany me down to central booking."

"I appreciate it, Detective."

"Anytime, Cat Woman, anytime."

I had done all I could for the moment. Now I had to wait till tomorrow.

It turned out to be a long night. I couldn't sleep. Tony prescribed the time-tested remedy for that—making love. I said I'd pass, I just didn't want to. But neither did I want him to leave. So he ended up sleeping in my bed. I ended up on the sofa. And the put-upon cats roamed all night from one room to the other.

I thought morning would never come. But of course it did, and Basillio and I went out for breakfast. I ordered poached eggs on buttered whole wheat toast and he had pancakes and bacon, starting a minor fight with me because I wouldn't sacrifice one of my eggs to be dumped onto his flapjacks. We returned to the apartment and glared at each other for about thirty minutes. I chalked it up to sexual tension.

At eleven I left the apartment and started the long, cold walk down to Centre Street. I arrived ten minutes late—a last-minute phone call had delayed me—and Rothwax was standing behind the frankfurter wagon where we always meet, when we do meet. He was griping bitterly between bites.

"The least you can do is be on time, C.W."

"I'm really sorry, Rothwax. I didn't get a wink of sleep last night and I guess I'm . . . It just isn't going very well with this man I . . . The lights were against me."

He sighed forgiveness wearily.

"What do you have for me?" I asked.

"Nothing very interesting. Three of them weren't in the system under anything but driver's license and state taxes."

"But one was," I crowed triumphantly, "and her name is Miranda Bly!"

"Nope. You're dead wrong on that one, Cat Woman. The only one with a police connection is Elizabeth Stimson."

"*Beth?*"

"Right. Arrested for prostitution, Southampton, Long Island, 1974."

"You must be joking!"

"Computer don't joke, C.W. The charges were dropped. She paid a twenty-five-dollar fine for misdemeanor loitering. The end." Rothwax laughed at me then. "Better close your mouth, Alice. You're going to start catching flies."

When I'd recovered from the news about Beth, I offered to pay for his hot dog.

"No," he said. "You owe me, all right. But not now." And then he trotted off.

But I didn't move a hair. I stood rooted to that spot, feeling too stupid to come in out of the rain that had begun to sweep in off the river.

21

Like the proverbial fly in amber, we were stuck in molasses-thick traffic on the endless stretch of highway. We were driving in a car Tony had borrowed from his friend Greg Roman, and the strong winter sun was right in our eyes.

Basillio jerked violently at the knot in his tie. "This is why all fathers give their sons two pieces of indisputable advice," said Tony. "One: Never eat the chile in a diner. Two: *Never* get on the Long Island Expressway."

Only half listening to Tony' complaints, I was staring down at that twenty-year-old photograph of Beth Stimson, part of the mysterious group of items I'd discovered in Will Gryder's room up at Covington.

Tony went on grumbling. "I don't understand this! We shouldn't have any traffic at all now. We're going in the wrong direction at the right time. The traffic is supposed to be going *into* the city this time of morning, not out to the east end of the Island."

"Where are we now?" I finally asked.

"Just at the Nassau-Suffolk line. Route 110. We've got at least another forty-five minutes to go on this road."

"Oh. Well, I'm sorry we're stuck, but thank

you for helping me, Tony. Really. I have, I am afraid, been maltreating you."

"Mal-treating." He repeated the word, giving it a kind of Jack Nicholson inflection with a smile to match. "What a beautiful word you just used." He leaned over and kissed me, obviously constrained by his suit and tie.

We were both in, as Tony had dubbed it earlier, "yuppie drag." I had borrowed Mrs. Oshrin's fur jacket, and under it I wore one of those female Wall Streeter suits with a string tie on my white silk shirt. I'd purchased it at a discount house in 1984 and had worn it only once before: when I was despairing of ever making a decent living from acting, and had applied for a job as head of the theater department at an expensive and very arty girls' school upstate. I didn't get the position.

The car moved ahead a few inches.

"Maybe," Tony speculated, "all these people are driving out to the Island to buy their Thanksgiving turkeys."

"They raise ducks out on Long Island, Tony, not turkeys. And I don't think there are many duck farms left."

"Well, maybe they're on the way to their summer places in the Hamptons."

"It's November, Basillio! November!"

I saw the merest hint of a smile on his lips then. That was me—gullible old Alice. Always ready to snap at the bait of one of Basillio's dumb put-ons.

At last the traffic was beginning to thin out. Tony maneuvered us into the speed lane and we started to move.

"Now don't forget who we are," I cautioned him.

"How the hell can I forget who we are?" he said huffily. "You're New York's finest unemployed middle-aged actress. And I'm the man without a family, a permanent place of residence, or a single prospect in the world. And of the two of us, I think you'll agree my story is sadder. At least some people know how good you are. But tell me when the last time was you heard it in the street that Tony Basillio is the most imaginative, gut-wrenching stage designer working in the business today?"

I let him ramble on. For a while. "I was talking about who we're supposed to be in the context of this little journey we're making today, Basillio—*today*."

"Oh, that. Yeah, I know who we are. We're writing a Sunday supplement piece on sex and sin in the Hamptons. Soon to appear in that nowhere little newspaper we work for: the *Nowhere Times-Mirror*."

"Not exactly. The *Manhattan Messenger*."

"And how sweet it is."

"Slow down, Tony. Here we are."

We exited from the Expressway and took Old Montauk Highway into the town of Southampton. What a lovely gem of a town it looked that early-winter morning, reeking of genteel, kindly money. And there were all kinds of parking spaces, which seemed to excite Tony more than the town itself. The shops were just opening for the day. After leaving the car, we found a small coffee place on the main street and went in.

"What now?" Tony asked when we'd finished our repast.

"Follow me," I said.

We walked one long block to a red-stone Victorian building which housed the Southampton library. Just next to it was a museum with a sculpture court.

The librarian was extremely attentive and professional as I explained that I needed issues of the local newspapers dating back to early spring or late winter of 1974.

She then told me that the library held local papers only for a week or so. They didn't keep a back issue file of any kind. Since the information I wanted was from 1974, she suggested I go to the editorial offices of the *Southampton Star*, because in 1974 it was the only daily paper of record for the area.

The offices weren't far from the library— unassuming quarters on the floor above a dress shop. A thin little man in a red V-neck sweater heard me out patiently, and then informed me that, unhappily, while they did retain back issues, they had nothing earlier than 1981, as the files, and indeed the entire old office, had been destroyed in a 1980 fire.

I stomped down the stairs, feeling there was some demonic plot against me.

"Where next?" Tony asked. He looked so forlorn and out-of-character in that suit. His dress overcoat flapped about wildly in the cold wind.

"Don't worry," I said, straightening his tie. "I'll make this up to you."

"Where have I heard that one before?"

I shrugged. "Let's go to the police station."

We hurried along the near-empty streets until we reached the municipal building, half of which housed the Southampton Police Department. Two patrol cars painted in garish purple and yellow were stationed in front of the building. The station house was empty except for one officer, who was seated at a folding table stapling some reports. He was a young man with a bristle-brush haircut and a heavily starched uniform. He did not look happy in his work.

I knew full well that he had noticed us come in, but he absolutely refused to look up at us until I said loudly, "Excuse me, officer."

"Help you folks?" he asked.

Behind me, Tony muttered, "I ain't no folk. Are you?"

I silenced him with a quick backward jab from the heel of my shoe.

While I was explaining to the officer that I wanted information on an almost twenty-year-old prostitution arrest, he went on stapling. I finished my presentation and smiled pleasantly at the top of his head.

Instead of a reply, however, I received a mercilessly appraising look from him. And then Basillio got the same treatment. He let us know that we'd both come up short.

But finally he spoke. "Just what kind of information are you talking about?"

"The name of an arresting officer, for instance," I said. "The circumstances and time of the arrest— just general information."

He drove a staple home with great force then. "We don't give out things like that," he said briskly, "unless you're the lawyer representing the accused."

"But there *is* no accused, officer. As I said, the arrest occurred in 1974. And no, I'm not a lawyer, but—"

"Obviously you're not," he said, cutting me off. "Or you'd know the statute of limitations on a charge like that expired long ago."

"Yes, I know. I don't want to contest the charges, I'm only researching—"

"Can't help you, miss. Try the county seat—in Riverhead. We ship the closed files there. Maybe they have it, maybe they don't. Can't help you— and if I could, I wouldn't."

Basillio took a step forward then, but I stepped in front of him again.

"And why wouldn't you?" I said, looking into his grinning face.

"Because storming in here and demanding things is not the way it's done. Not around here. Understand?"

Storming? Demanding? Had I done that? Had this case turned me into some kind of a shrew who alienated total strangers? I turned to Basillio and started to put that very question to him.

"Time to go, Swede," he said, taking my arm. "We only *think* we're in the Hamptons. It's really the Village of the Damned."

We found our way back to the coffee shop where we'd initiated our visit to the charming town. The waitress, a pretty young girl with long red hair, greeted us warmly.

"Cold out there, isn't it?"

We took the same table and Tony ordered another coffee and another muffin bursting its little paper jacket with cranberries and nuts.

"Not our day, eh, Sherlock?" he asked as he began to ladle on the butter.

I had to agree. I was frustrated and angry, and the wholesome smell of fresh bread was making me gag. The town library had nothing. The files at the newspaper office had been burned to a crisp. Then the big finish: that nasty young cop with the chip on his shoulder—an unhappy little bureaucrat.

"I can't see why this is so important," Tony said, his mouth full of muffin, jam painting his lips.

"Well, it is important. It's damn important to me." The RETRO computer was generally a whiz, I had to admit. But how did I know the police hadn't made a mistake that night? Maybe Beth had just had a bit too much to drink at a party and gone off with someone. Maybe it was a simple one-night stand, and someone mistook it for soliciting. Maybe she'd lent her ID to another girl for the night. I had to be sure.

"So she was young and stupid and she turned a trick," Tony said. "It happens."

I ignored him. I had to think. What next? *Who* next?

Tony had finished half of his second breakfast. "Well, what now?" he asked. He was holding the paper coffee cup in both hands and seemed to be looking over my shoulder.

"We need another source," I answered him.

"Right, right . . . obviously," he said distractedly.

I saw then that he was following the young waitress's every move with his eyes.

His glance was so predatory that I said caustically, "You'd like to take her to a motel right now, wouldn't you, Basillio?"

He pulled his eyes away, looking caught. "Now, now, Swede."

Had the "john's" eyes followed young Beth

that night in the same hungry way? If indeed it *was* our Beth. And what in the world would make a beautiful young violinist turn a trick in a place like Southampton? Had she been stranded out here? Did she need a place to sleep?

My goodness! I flung my hands up in exasperation at my own denseness. A place to sleep. A motel!

Tony looked at me with alarm. Oh, I was stupid not to have thought of it before. If she did do what they said, and was arrested for it, it had to have happened in a public place. Like a motel. That was were this arrest had to have occurred.

I caught the waitress's eye and beckoned her over.

"Are there any motels close by?" I asked her.

She smiled, understanding, or in this case, misunderstanding, that Basillio and I were eager lovers looking for a room. "Sure," she said. "A lovely one about five blocks from here, nearer to the water. But it's a little expensive."

"Is it a new place?"

"Fairly new."

"What about an old one? Is there one around that was in business as early as 1974?"

Understandably, she looked at me as if this demand for a motel of a particular vintage was odd. "Well, yeah. The Dolphin Inn. By the municipal building. But you don't want to go there—it's a fleabag."

"The municipal building—you mean where the police station is?"

"Right."

How strange. Tony and I had just come from there, and we hadn't seen a motel.

I thanked her and hustled Basillio out of there without allowing him to finish muffin number two.

We walked past the police department entrance. A cobblestone alley adjoined the building. Tony pointed up at a decrepit sign nailed to the trunk of a sycamore tree: DOLPHIN MOTOR INN. DAILY RATES. TV.

We followed the winding alley, and suddenly looming up in front of us was an ancient two-tiered wooden structure with perhaps ten rooms on each landing. At the edge of the ground floor was an office. There were only two cars parked in the guest spaces.

The office was a gray old place with sticky linoleum. An elderly woman in multiple sweaters sat on a high stool behind the counter, turning the pages of her newspaper with gnarled fingers poking out of fingerless gloves. She shoved the paper aside and put on her welcoming face as soon as she spotted us at the door.

"How're you folks today? Need a nice room?"

"We're not exactly looking for a room. . . ." I began.

"Not looking for a room at this very moment, that is," Basillio interrupted me, "but we'd like to make a little down payment on one." Tony placed a twenty-dollar bill on the counter, and the lady had it in one of her many pockets before I could even blink.

"We're planning to stay here on our honeymoon," Tony told the woman. "That's so you'll remember us."

"You be sure of that, young man," she said, picking up her burning cigarette from a make-shift ashtray fashioned from tinfoil.

I allowed Basillio to take hold of my hand and keep it in his, while I resumed speaking to the old lady. "Actually, what we need today is some information about something that happened here in town about twenty years ago."

"Try me. Not much I don't know."

"Well, I think a young girl was arrested here—in this motel—for prostitution," I said haltingly. "The year was 1974." The words had come out all wrong. It sounded as though I was accusing her of running the kind of place where such an arrest was routine. I yearned to begin again. But it was too late.

To my surprise, though, she didn't seem insulted. "Oh, my," she said indulgently. "Can't say I remember the particulars, but if it was something like that, it had to be Hy up to his old tricks."

"Who is Hy?"

She shook her head. "Old Hiram Kenally. Rest his soul. He had a . . . weakness . . . for the girls. For the *young* girls, if you know what I mean. Not that my husband or I had anything to do with that sort of thing, but we figured what Hy Kenally did was his business. He was quite the regular here at the Dolphin—he and his lady friends. The thing was, his wife Vera always seemed to know exactly what he was up to. She'd wait and time it perfect, and just when Hy and his friend were . . . well, Vera seemed to get a kick out of calling the police on them. We had a ruckus going on here many a night, I'll tell you. It got to be pretty silly."

"I take it Mr. Kenally is dead," I said.

"Long dead. More than ten years. And Vera went the next year. They were something, the two of them Funny part is, I think she really loved that old bastard. Had've been my husband, I'd have killed him long before his heart did."

I brought out the little photograph of Beth Stimson then. "Do you recognize this girl as one of the ones Mr. Kenally brought here?"

She took a brief look at the picture. "Not really. But I never took that much notice. Besides, my husband was probably the one on-duty the night she was here. He worked nights more than me."

"Would it be possible to speak to him?"

"Be a pretty good trick if you could. Bill passed away too."

"I'm sorry," I said. "I don't suppose you'd know anyone else who might talk to us about the arrest? Anyone who'd remember what happened?"

"Well," she said slowly, "I guess you could try Tom Scott. He's the one who usually came to pick up Hy and the girl. He retired from the force a while ago. But he still lives out here, in Bridgehampton. It's not far."

"Think he'd talk to us?"

"I don't see why not, honey. But with Tom, who knows? He's about as nuts as Hy was. Spends all his time fooling around with old wrecks instead of other people. Probably do him good to see two human beings for a change."

She wrote down the directions to Mr. Scott's home for us. I thanked her profusely, and Tony said something to her I couldn't hear. Whatever it was, it made her laugh. "See you soon!" she called out as we left.

We followed her driving instructions carefully: East to Bridgehampton, north along the main street, past the war memorial—though we couldn't see which war was being memorialized—turn left, and two miles on, look for a little gray house.

The place was easy to spot. It was as the innkeeper had said—strewn with old cars.

"Oh, brother," Tony sighed. "Do you suppose that's Tom Scott?" He meant the lanky man in shirtsleeves leaning against a fender, calmly smoking a cigarette. "He looks about as friendly as Dan Duryea."

We parked just off the road, then got out and approached the tough old man cautiously.

"Mr. Scott?" I inquired.

After a long, critical look at us, he touched the brim of the baseball cap turned backward on his head. "The very one," he said.

"Nice to meet you. My name is Alice Nestleton."

I might just as well have announced that I was an extraterrestrial. He waited for me to go on.

"Mr. Scott, I was wondering if I could talk to you about an arrest you made years ago, in 1974."

"Who sent you out here?"

"The proprietress of the Dolphin Inn in Southampton."

"That old bat always did have a big mouth."

I thought perhaps he was waiting for us to laugh. But we didn't, and he fell silent again. Obviously he had no intention of inviting us inside, and no curiosity about our reason for being there. I decided to dispense with the cover story about our being journalists, to just tell the truth to this wiry old policeman and hope for the best.

"Mr. Scott, I'm an investigator looking into a murder—and frankly, time is short. I believe that one of the suspects was a young girl you arrested on a prostitution charge at the Dolphin in 1974. The man involved may have been someone named Hiram Kenally. I realize it was eighteen years ago, but . . . this was the girl." I held the photo up close to his face. "Does she look at all familiar to you?"

He didn't look at it.

"Half the prostitution arrests I ever made had to do with that idiot Kenally."

"Please look at the picture."

He studied it for a minute. "Looks familiar."

"Is it possible the whole thing was a mistake?"

"Mistake!" He grunted. "That old bastard with his pants around his ankles was a mistake, I guess."

"So you *are* sure you saw the girl there?"

"Had on nothing but her socks. A mistake, yeah! That's what *she* claimed. Guess those six twenty-dollar bills on the dresser were a mistake, too. Arrogant little twist, she was. She had the gall to threaten to sue me for false arrest." Scott laughed nastily then. "Old Kenally had the nerve to deny it, too. I let the two of them bitch all they wanted to. I still took them in. Guess he thought his money could actually change what *is* real to what *ain't* real. You'd think he'd get tired of playing the john after a while, but not that old bastard. Heard he even died with his pants down. They found him out in Montauk with a fourteen-year-old from one of the migrant camps."

"Sounds like a real sweet guy," Tony said under his breath.

"Mr. Scott," I said, "can you tell me what happened after you took them out of the Dolphin Inn?"

"Happened? What do you mean, 'what happened'? What usually happened. He was *Mr.* Hiram Kenally. They were released. She got off on a misdemeanor loitering charge. Twenty-bucks fine, or something. Walked off to turn another trick."

"And what about the money you saw? Wasn't that rather a lot for Mr. Kenally to spend on a prostitute?"

"You didn't know that bastard. If he had three dollars in his pocket, he'd pay three. If the charge was three thousand, he'd have paid that just as easy. Whatever it took.

"Now, as for you investigating a murder, lady."—he flicked his cigarette away brutally—"I don't know whether I believe a single word of it."

"I can appreciate your position, Mr. Scott. But the important question is, can *I* believe *you*?"

He didn't answer. He only spat onto the frozen ground, and then drifted into his house.

I walked back to the car slowly. Tony climbed in and asked what our next stop would be.

"Nowhere just yet, Tony. Let's just sit here a while and get warm."

"What is it, Swede?" he asked, concern in his voice.

"Well, that's it, isn't it? That's what I was after. Tom Scott just confirmed everything. Little Beth turned a trick with a dirty old man for a hundred and twenty dollars."

"Yeah. Just like the computer said. But what does it mean? It's just the way of the world, isn't it?"

"Not the world of the Riverside String Quartet—not the one I witnessed just last month. And you know, Tony, Southampton is a very small world, isn't it?"

"What do you mean by that?"

"I mean, if Beth was plying her trade out here, then why not in Manhattan? Why be so specialized? And I also mean, what if she wasn't the only one? What if Miranda did it too—and Darcy—and Roz? In fact, maybe that rich old Aunt Sarah wasn't a Scottish Fold cat at all."

"So do you think the stolen cats had nothing to do with anything?" Tony asked.

"What I think, Tony, is that we'd better come up with some tricks of our own. And like I said, time is short."

22

Will Gryder was in his shallow grave in some restful spot in southern California.

The Riverside String Quartet was no more.

The clock was ticking.

The egg was broken.

Now it was time to make the omelet.

I sat waiting for Tony to return from the mission I'd sent him out on. Bushy and I were tossing the catnip ball around, just to pass time. I was singing an old standard that I'd recast to fit my feline preoccupations: "I Want a Tabby Kind of Love."

The doorbell sounded then.

"Here comes Tony," I told Bushy on my way to the door. "Getting excited?"

He walked off slowly but firmly, the ball in his teeth.

Basillio's jacket seemed to give off the scent of the cold outdoors. "Well, here the filthy things are," he said, dropping a paper sack filled with books onto the sofa. "Do me a favor, will you, and never send me over there again."

"Oh, come on, Basillio. I thought you'd enjoy being in the Forty-second Street area. I thought it would bring back fond memories of your dark and misspent youth."

His face took on a grim, wounded expression. "I do not like browsing in pornographic bookstores for tawdry paperbacks about prostitutes. It demeans my serious erotic feelings for you."

"Such high-flown language from you, Basillio."

"Here," he said, stepping up to me and encircling my waist, "let me put it to you . . . in . . . ah . . . layman's terms."

I laughed. "Later, Tony."

I looked down at the things he'd tossed onto the sofa: five identical copies of some trash entitled *Hookers*. The book was about a hundred and fifty pages in length, printed on cheap stock and purporting to be actual case studies of "working girls."

The cover design was suitably lurid, showing the grotesque sexual posturings of three over-endowed women in various states of undress.

Tony picked up one of the copies.

"Isn't that amazing?" he said. "These things haven't changed in the past twenty years! They just keep recycling the same covers."

"So much the better," I said. "Both the cover and the title. I sent you out for something on prostitution, but I never thought you'd find something called *Hookers*. It's absolutely perfect."

Carefully, I began to rip the cover off each of the books.

"What the hell are you doing?" he asked, astonished.

"You'll see in a minute."

I gathered the five covers and brought them to the dining room table, Tony following in my footsteps.

"Well, you've been a busy bee, haven't you?" he said, looking over my shoulder at the five stamped envelopes laid out on the table. Each was addressed to a member of the Riverside String Quartet, the last one to Mathew Hazan at his West Fifty-seventh Street office.

"And just what are these—your show-and-tell homework?" Tony had picked up a couple of the five-color xeroxes I had had made from an old *Scientific American*.

"What do they look like?"

"Pictures of mice."

"Exactly. Tufted field mice. Some of the world's most adaptable creatures, particularly when they displace house mice. The way they did at Covington."

Tony folded his arms and began what can only be described as a peculiar little dance. He circled the chair I sat in, looking at me from different angles. He appeared to be making some kind of mock evaluation of me.

"I think, Miss Nestleton," he pronounced, "that the years of scratching out a living—the endless hard times—have finally taken their toll on you. In other words, you have finally cracked, baby."

"Hardly," I said. "You'll see."

I picked up my scissors and cut out the five tufted little creatures from their verdant backgrounds. Then, on the back of each *Hookers* cover, I affixed one of the mice with Scotch tape. Finally, I popped each cover into one of the neatly typed envelopes.

"I think the clouds are beginning to clear a bit," Tony said. "You're about to play a little game of post office, aren't you?"

"That's right. A *serious* game of post office. One of the five people who are going to get this cryptic greeting card is the murderer. I want that person to be confused about whether the sender is friend or foe.

"I want that person to feel that the sender knows a lot about a lot of things. About the Dolphin Inn in Southampton, for instance."

"You mean you want them to think they're about to be blackmailed?"

"Well, no . . . and yes. I want them to look at the card as both a reminder and a threat. Because what it's really saying is that they had better get up to where the tufted field mice play and find Will's manuscript. Because it's still hidden there: somewhere at the Covington Center for the Arts."

"But, Swede, you have the manuscript, what there is of it. The outline only hints at an exposé, and Gryder never mentions prostitution specifically."

"He was murdered before he could. And besides, the murderer doesn't know how far Will had gotten on the book. Only you and I know that—and Ford Donaldson."

Tony watched me silently as I sealed each letter. When I'd finished, he asked me rather gravely, "Are you really going to mail those things?"

"Yes, of course I am."

He shook his head. "I don't know, Swede. To be honest, it seems to me that you kind of blew it up there with that state cop and that first trap of yours. And now you're clutching at straws. And I mean *clutching*."

"We'll see."

"So you're really going to mail them?"

"Yes, I *really* am—that is to say, we are. But not from here. From Northampton. So that the killer knows this anonymous correspondent knows whereof he or she speaks."

Tony slammed his hand down on the table. Bushy flew out of the room. Pancho flew in.

"*Now* I know why you wanted me to hang on to Greg's old heap, even after we got back from Southampton! Damn! I should have known you had something up your sleeve."

I gently smoothed back the hair on poor Tony's head. "I knew you'd love being in the country with us for a few days.'

"Us?" he asked.

"Yes. Me and Pancho and Bushy."

"God."

"You're looking very pale, Basillio. Some sun and some fresh country air will do you a world of good. We'll walk in the woods, roast chestnuts, maybe—"

"Get killed by a killer," he finished for me.

"We're not going to be killed, Tony. Besides, I can't put these in the mail until I check something out up there. A white duffel bag with a broken lock."

"What's in it?"

"Nothing."

He was silent for a few beats, unwilling to delve further. Then he asked, "Wouldn't you rather go to Atlantic City?"

"Basillio, you're going to love it up there. Covington is wonderful. It absolutely reeks of dreams."

"Dreams? What dreams?"

"Artists' dreams. Great ennobling projects."

"Like 'Still Life of Piano Player with Chisel in Chest'?"

"Not exactly. But that's a good title."

"This case is making you macabre as well as crazy, Swede. I really hope you know what you're doing."

Did I? Did I *really*?

"Didn't you leave something out of that stuff we're going to be doing up in the country?" Tony asked. "Aren't we going to make insane love in front of a roaring fire?"

"Aren't you going to help me catch Pancho and get him in the carrier?"

"Why don't you just hold up a picture of a tufted field mouse near the door?"

"Pancho is far too busy to hunt," I said.

We began to stalk the wily Pancho. He was, oddly enough, quiet once he was inside the box. Bushy, on the other hand, walked right in, cooperating fully, only to metamorphose into a shrieking holy terror as soon as the lock had clamped shut.

So many contradictions. So little time.

23

Oh, I'd seen this road before. I knew where the rest stops were, and where to get the cheapest gas. But this time Tony was at the wheel. And he spent the bulk of the time muttering and bitching and asking himself why, how, he'd once again allowed me to talk him into some nutty undertaking against his better judgment.

The cats glowered at us from their prison cells on the backseat, their eyes huge and iridescent in the darkness.

It got colder with every mile, and once we had crossed the state line into Massachusetts, freezing mists disabled our vision no matter how hard we worked the defroster. I thought perhaps all parties might be soothed by a few choruses of one of the good old hymns, so I launched into "Nearer My God to Thee." I soon gave up on that, though.

It was around eleven in the evening when we pulled into the courtyard of the small hotel in Northampton.

"Can't this mysterious white duffel bag wait until tomorrow morning?" Tony asked, after we'd checked in and released Bushy and Pancho into their new environment. The room smelled faintly of insect spray, and the cats were wandering around sniffing suspiciously at every corner.

"We have to go now, Tony. It's no more than twenty minutes away. And then we can come right back. Maybe we can get something to eat in town, although it's a bit late."

"Maybe there's an all-night record store, too. Think we can find one of those?"

"What do you need with a record store?"

"I don't know. Just asking."

Basillio is very peculiar when he's angry. Very peculiar indeed.

I poured fresh litter into a big cardboard box and set it in the bathtub, cautioning the cats against starting any trouble while we were gone. Then Tony and I headed for Covington.

The house and grounds were deserted, and still as death. I guided Tony down the access road toward the studio where Will had died, away from the main house, until we could go no further. Then, grasping my flashlight tightly, I walked toward the creek, Tony following. The wind was powerful and relentless. There was no moon.

I pushed in the door to the shed and stood there for a full minute. Basillio's rapid breathing sounded like the roar of the ocean in my ear. Without putting on the light, we made our way to the narrow aisle and turned down it, to the place where Ford Donaldson and I had set our trap.

The white duffel was still there.

"Looks like somebody got here before you," Tony said.

He was right. The bag had been shredded

with a knife and ripped open. The sundry papers and trash I'd stuffed inside it were strewn about on the floor, as if a pack rat had been clawing through it.

"Well, too bad," he said.

"Too bad? It's beautiful, Tony! It confirms everything. Don't you see what happened? After my trap was exposed as bogus and the quartet unceremoniously kicked me out of their midst, one of them came back here and searched this bag, looking for Gryder's evidence—for his manuscript."

I felt so good that, had there been a few more inches of space in that cramped aisle, I might have executed a most unladylike jig.

"You see, Tony, the trap wasn't really bogus. I just baited it incorrectly. With those wee Scottish kittens."

"Let's talk about this over dinner," he said. "It's freezing in here."

We returned to the car and drove to the stately old post office in town. I dropped the five envelopes into the mailbox just in front of the building.

I got behind the wheel and, by instinct, found the little diner where Ford Donaldson had taken me for coffee. Whatever it was they fed us had plenty of good-tasting gravy on top of it. I even had lemon pie for dessert. It was nearly one in the morning when we returned to the hotel. The cats were fine. I opened two cans of food, overfeeding them as a kind of bribe. Tony stretched out on the bed and was fast asleep in a matter of seconds, fully clothed. I covered him with a blanket, and after changing into my wooly red nightshirt I lay down beside him, listening to the window shivering in its casement.

I awoke at seven-thirty. Tony had gone.

There was a note saying he would bring back breakfast, provided he didn't get lost.

I showered, then made the bed, forgetting that there was maid service here. I guess I had forgotten to tell Tony that all we had to do was go downstairs anytime after eight A.M. and breakfast would be served to us. The cats were holding up remarkably well, not complaining much at all, and I made sure to tell them how much I appreciated it. Then I put in a call to Ford Donaldson.

He had come in to the office early and was genuinely surprised to hear from me, even more surprised to find I was in a nearby hotel. I didn't want to discuss matters on the phone, so I asked him bluntly if he'd mind driving over to see me as soon as possible.

For a long time, there was no answer. In fact, I thought the line had gone dead. But then he asked with no small amount of suspicion, "What brings you back out this way, Alice?"

"I'd rather tell you that in person."

"What about a hint?"

"If you could just spare me a few minutes, Ford. For old time's sake," I added.

Again, he hesitated. "Look ... I'll just drop over now."

"Fine. I'll be waiting."

I wished I had that coffee Basillio was bringing. I jumped when I heard a sudden noise. But it was only Pancho knocking over the wastepaper basket and sticking his face in it for a quick look. "Just behave yourself, Panch," I told him, "and I'll get you sardines for lunch." I could tell he didn't believe me.

In less that ten minutes Ford was knocking at the door. He stepped in quickly, as if there were something illicit in his visit. His eyes roamed over the room professionally, taking everything in.

"I'm here with a friend," I said, noticing that he had fixed on Tony's shaving kit.

"Glad to hear it." Then he smiled, sort of, leaned heavily against the dresser, and asked: "What can I do for you, Alice?"

"Won't you sit for a moment?" I said.

"Better not. I can't stay long."

"Ford, how's the investigation going?"

He shrugged. "Not good."

"Did you know the quartet has broken up?"

"What?"

"The Riverside String Quartet. They've announced that they're disbanding."

"That's a shame. But it's not like it's the Everly Brothers or something."

I sat down on the only chair in the room. He watched my movements carefully, like a mouse watches a cat. Or a cat a mouse.

"Listen, Ford, in light of everything that's happened, this is hard to say. But I'll just come out and say it. I need your help—again."

His eyes darted around. "Well, if it's tourist information you're after, I can recommend some lovely places to visit. You and your friend like covered bridges?"

"Listen to me, Lieutenant Donaldson. In about three days' time, the person who murdered Will Gryder is going to break into the house at the Covington colony."

"Well, thank you for that tip." His sarcasm was like a weight.

"And I want you to be there—with me—when that happens."

He smiled, shook his head, and moved one foot on the floorboards as if he were stubbing out a cigarette.

"You're not serious—are you?"

"Totally."

"You mean you want to do that whole dance again, Alice?"

"I did make a mistake. But this time there *is* no mistake."

His smile turned up a notch and I saw him grind his teeth—the giveaway signs that he was trying not to blow his stack. "You did a little more than make a mistake, Alice," he said. "You pretty much made a fool out of me. And my department. And things were going bad enough as it was."

"Did you go back to that shed at any time?" I asked.

"No. Why should I?"

"Someone shredded the duffel bag we planted."

"So?"

"Can I just tell you what I've learned over the past few days about how Beth—"

"Hey! Listen, lady ... I don't want to hear anything you have to say about the Will Gryder case. Understand? You got me involved in some kind of dingbat sting operation. I bought it off you once. But that won't happen a second time. I don't care how good-looking you are—or how persuasive. You *are* persuasive, you know ... but so are a lot of crazy people."

"Ford, I promise you no one will be made a fool of this time."

"You got that one right." His face hardened into a blank. "Nice to see you again, Alice. Enjoy your stay."

He opened the door.

I stood up. "Ford! Please wait!"

"I don't think so, Alice," he called over his shoulder, still moving.

I had expected skepticism from him. That was logical. After all, he had been burned once. But I hadn't expected this kind of overt antagonism.

"Please listen!" I said again in the doorway. He stopped and turned then. But I could think of nothing to say that would spark his interest in my plan. I could think of nothing, period. I was living out the classic actor's nightmare: not a single word came to mind. Ford didn't wait there very long. I watched him disappear down the staircase.

Just as Donaldson pulled out of the gravel parking lot, Tony drove up in the dusty borrowed car. He came into the room carrying enough breakfast for six people: coffee, donuts, egg sandwiches, rolls, bacon and sausages in tin foil. He place a towel over the large overturned suitcase and laid out his feast.

Over coffee, I told Tony about Donaldson's visit and his refusal to help.

"So what do you want to do now?" he asked, sounding strangely detached.

"We have to do it ourselves."

"Do what?"

"Wait for the murderer, Tony. Trap the murderer!"

"Oh, but of course." He laughed. "Where do we wait?"

"In the car. Behind the main house at Covington."

"And this cop Donaldson doesn't want in on it? What the hell's the matter with that guy? You must be losing your charms, Swede."

"Ford doesn't think much of my charms, or my methods either."

"I can't believe it! Didn't you tell him about the mouse cut-outs, or any of that neat stuff with the book covers? I mean, once he heard about *Hookers*, he'd know how scientific your investigative methods are. Call him up now and tell him, Swede. He'll be back here like a shot."

I sipped my coffee, not rising to the bait. For some reason, my traps really offended Tony. They offend a lot of people. But I'm just one person: If I had the financial backing and the resources and personnel a police department has, I'd be able to pull off much more elaborate stings. I wouldn't have to send out trick postcards. I could conduct large-scale surveillance operations.

But I have none of those things. And I never will. So I have to work quickly and inexpensively and target every move I make right at the heart of the matter—live by my wits. If I have to use whimsy or intuition or anything else that works—fine. Besides, what I've found is that a simple postcard will often flush out a murderer, while around-the-clock surveillance and sophisticated listening devices can miss the mark completely. My cards to the members of the quartet were a kind of performance art, and that's why I knew they would work.

But how was one to explain that to a Ford Donaldson, pro that he was, or to a Tony Basillio, rogue stage designer?

So I overlooked Tony's nasty comments and dedicated myself to being the sweetest girl in the world to him. We spent the next couple of days being tourists in old New England. We drove out to see Nathaniel Hawthorne's house. We visited the Impressionist Art Museum in Williamstown, and looked at the shuttered summer playhouse there. We walked in the woods. We dined in the romantic little inn near Great Barrington and went back to our low-budget hotel and made extraordinarily sweet love at night.

Then, as the daylight vanished on the third day, our tourist impersonation ended. I had never seen Basillio so depressed.

We drove to the Covington colony and parked at the back of the main house, behind the kitchen, so that we would be invisible to anyone entering the premises through the front gate.

It was five forty-one in the evening. We had taken along a big thermos filled with black coffee, and we had plenty of cheese and bread and cookies from the gourmet shop in town. I still had Ford Donaldson's flashlight from that night we'd "trapped" Miranda Bly in the shed, and Tony had brought his Walkman with its earphones.

As we settled into the front seat of the car, Tony whispered close to my ear: "I don't know what the hell I'm doing here, but I'll defend to the death your right to make me do it."

It was a terribly cold night. Running the heater would have instantly tipped anyone on the premises to our presence. So we sat in the freezing car, just waiting.

"Tomorrow night I won't forget the blankets," I said sheepishly to Basillio, who had not spoken to me for hours. I heard him chuckle bitterly as he sat with his hands tucked into his armpits. His cackling seemed to go on and on.

By midnight we had finished the coffee and the food. I was listening to the all-night classical musical station on the small radio, while Tony dozed. At one-thirty they announced the next selection: Schumann's String Quartet No. 5, featuring the Riverside String Quartet as recorded live at a 1982 performance. It was so bizarre I had to wake Tony to report it.

Around two-thirty he announced quietly, "I think I'm beginning to hate you, Swede."

"No, you aren't."

He squirmed. "We have no business being out here. We should be in a warm bed in Manhattan."

"We'll wait till three-thirty tonight. Just another hour."

"And tomorrow night?"

"The same."

He groaned.

"You can't be losing heart, Tony. We just started."

"I never had any heart for this adventure. Only for you."

"Not an 'adventure,' Basillio. Bad choice of word. I'm too old for adventures."

"Well, then 'hubris.' "

"Whose hubris?"

"Yours, Swede. You can't stand to lose. I

mean, you can't stand to lose your superiority in things criminal."

"That's nonsense."

"It isn't. No one's going to get the bone away from you. The more you're thwarted and insulted, the more obstinate you become, the more you worry the bone. And that's why directors hate to work with you, too."

"Is that the reason?"

"*Exactly* the reason. You're so busy with the bone that you lose sight of the real goal. You stop thinking, and all kinds of fantasies take over. And you do nothing to quash them."

"So you think this enterprise is a fantasy, do you?"

"I hope it isn't. But it is a fantasy that the Riverside String Quartet is an evil entity."

"Did I ever say that?"

"You didn't say it, but you believe it. Otherwise we wouldn't be sitting here freezing in the middle of the night on this godforsaken farm."

"It's not a *farm*, Tony! It's an artists' colony." I knew that wasn't much of a comeback, but I thought it best to stop the argument there.

I turned away from him and stared out of the car window. The night seemed sordid and threatening. It didn't feel like being in the country.

Well, no matter what Tony thought, I knew it wasn't just "hubris" that was driving me on. They *had* thwarted and insulted me, though, and I wouldn't forget it soon.

We got back to the hotel at four in the morning and fell asleep immediately, thankful at least for the warmth.

The next night we were better prepared. We

brought blankets and several thermoses, one with soup, and a lot more snacks, plus a deck of cards. The first couple of hours on the stakeout, as they say, were oddly pleasant. Until we started to play casino.

We had to rig up a flashlight so that it illuminated the cards between us on the seat, but not the car. We managed it with a blanket finally, but it made sitting there very uncomfortable. It had been more than fifteen years since I'd played a game of casino, and I had to have my memory refreshed as to the rules. Tony was little help, however, because he remembered even less than I. We got into a fight over the method of scoring. I knew there were eleven points in a game. And I knew the ten of diamonds counted for two and the two of spades was a point, and each ace was one. So that meant "cards" and "spades" had to total four points, but we couldn't agree on the breakdown.

When we finally did come to an agreement, we commenced an intense game there in the car, in the freezing night, virtually under a tent, waiting for a killer.

I was winning handily. Then I decided to build fours. There was one on the table, so to speak, and I had two more in my hand. So I laid one of the fours from my hand on top of the one on the table and announced my intention to build.

Tony grinned, placed the two of spades on top of my four, and said he was building sixes.

I explained that he couldn't do that—it was against the rules.

He said he could.

Tempers flared. I picked up the two of spades

and threw it at him. He grabbed my hand. I had just raised my other hand when he suddenly put his finger to his lips, cautioning silence.

I had heard it, too. The sound of a motor—coming closer.

"I think a car's turning up the drive," Basillio said urgently.

I stiffened in my seat. We could see nothing. The house obscured our view just as efficiently as it hid us from sight.

"At least I think it was a car," Tony whispered. "I saw bright lights coming up the main road, and then they vanished. So it either stopped and turned out its lights or it turned out its lights and made a right turn onto this property."

I rolled down the window, in spite of the cold. "We'll know for sure in a few minutes," I said. "We should be able to see any lights on the ground floor." I strained toward the hulking structure of the house, but I heard nothing.

"There!" Tony said.

"Where?"

"It's gone now, but I saw something."

Then I could see it too: a beam of light inside the house on the ground floor, sweeping.

"He's in! He's in!" I said, and opened the car door. The two of us slipped out quietly.

"What do we do now?" Tony asked.

"Wait for him to leave, and grab him. He'll go up to Will's room and tear it apart. He'll find nothing. And then he'll leave. We'll be there."

We walked around to the entrance to the house, hunched against the cold. I took my place on one side of the door and motioned Tony to the other side. We were like freezing, frightened bookends. It was so dark that I couldn't even see the outline of the intruder's car.

I'm not sure how long we were waiting for the intruder to finish his search and give up. But it was long enough for me to realize I'd left the flashlight in the car. I wanted to run back for it, but didn't dare. It was long enough for me to develop an intensely painful cramp in my leg. The pain was so bad I must have groaned involuntarily.

"What's the matter?" Basillio hissed from his post.

There was no time to explain. The front door opened then, and a figure walked out.

"Stop him, Tony!"

He grabbed the figure, but it shook free and ran, Tony in pursuit.

Suddenly the area was flooded with light. Dazzling, diamond-white light. Tony froze in his tracks. The intruder stopped too, for a second, but then swung an object at Tony. It landed. Tony grunted.

"Don't move!" an authoritative voice boomed.

Now I could see the source of the light: the headlights of Ford Donaldson's vehicle. The lieutenant himself was standing by the driver's window, his weapon trained on the intruder. No one moved, except me. I walked over to Tony to see if he was okay. He had been hit by a leather pocketbook which now lay on the ground, its contents strewn about.

Ford walked closer, keeping his gun straight out. He looked over briefly at me. "I was just bringing you some coffee, Alice."

I was breathing too heavily to thank him

properly. I turned toward the intruder, now down on one knee.

"Stand up," Donaldson ordered, "and keep your hands over your head."

Slowly, the figure stood.

I took a good look. At first my brain registered nothing. The figure seemed familiar in a vague sort of way, but nothing actually clicked. Then Ford pulled the cap from the figure's head.

It was Mrs. Wallace. . . . My God, it was the cook, Mrs. Wallace!

She had cut her hair quite short and was wearing makeup and unisexual dark clothing. But there was no mistake about who it was.

I thought with dumb wonder: *But I didn't send her a postcard.*

Ford lowered the gun and walked past Mrs. Wallace, bending to examine the contents of her bag on the ground. After a few seconds, I heard him whistle long and low. When he straightened, he had a small object in his hand. He showed it to me. "This is one of the pieces of jewelry taken from Gryder's person. They said he won it at a piano competition in Belgium when he was just a kid. He came in third-place."

We all looked at the cook, who was staring hypnotically at the small ring. Her face seemed to be decomposing right before our eyes. Finally she burst into pitiful tears. "I couldn't . . . I couldn't destroy it," she wailed. "I got rid of everything else, but I just . . . couldn't. It was all that was left . . . it was so sad."

I put an arm around the trembling woman. "We know why you're here, Mrs. Wallace. You're in a lot of trouble. But you didn't murder Will Gryder . . . did you? But you know who did. You have to tell us everything, Mrs. Wallace. You have to think of yourself now."

She nodded through the tears.

Ford went to his car to bring the coffee he'd purchased for me.

We helped Mrs. Wallace back in through the doors of the old house and sat her in the chilly dining room, where she choked down the coffee and then began her story. She spoke in a racing, low voice, as if the words were fast unwinding from a spool.

"It was the 1970s, and all those girls wanted their careers. They wanted the money to finance the group bad—and they decided to do whatever they had to do to get it. They were all turning tricks, every one of them. But not like the whores on the street. Oh, no. Their johns were wealthy, and their fees were stiff. After all, these were beautiful young girls, educated, cultured—the stuff of fantasies for a lot of older men.

"The prostitution was Hazan's idea. But he didn't know where to begin. All he knew was how to book and manage small-time acts. He couldn't set up something like that by himself. So he looked for help.

"He called an old friend from the army—a man who was then a Broadway ticket-broker with some shady connections. Few people knew that this ticket-broker had a background as a pimp.

"The fifteen thousand in seed money was raised quickly enough. And the whoring stopped. But that's not something a woman forgets easily, even under the best circumstances. Most of the girls pulled through it all and started to put it behind them. But my poor little Rozalind had a harder time forgetting. She was . . . hurt . . . hurt badly . . . by a very sick man, a customer. She was lucky he didn't kill her, lucky not to lose her mind. But even she got over it, learned to forget, except for the fact that she couldn't ever have children, thanks to that sick man.

"So the years are moving on, and the quartet has become successful even beyond their own dreams. Then, at a social event, some charity thing for Carnegie Hall, the anonymous pimp, who'd gone on to make something of himself and is now a wealthy and respected business-man, meets the women for the first time. They know nothing about him. But he knows all about them, doesn't he? Anyway, he takes one look at that angel—Roz—and he's head-over-heels, hopelessly and forever in love. And soon they marry."

I touched the cook on the arm then, inter-rupting her narrative. "Are you saying the pimp was Benjamin Polikoff?!"

"Yes. Ben. He adored Roz. He became the most wonderful husband any woman could ever want. And a wonderful friend to the entire quar-tet. He made life great for her, and I know she loved him, too.

"But the love story doesn't end there, like in a fairy tale. Roz may have loved him dearly, but she was bored with him. She began to have af-fairs, most of them trifling. But then, there was Gryder. The affair with him was serious enough that she almost left Ben. But that one ended, too. Or so we thought. It wasn't really over, as Ben found out. Roz and Gryder went on seeing each other off and on for years—it never ended for them.

"You know all about the reason they came up here to rest. That trip to Europe was terrible for everybody. They were supposed to lay low here and play music. Then the visitors started arriving. And then one day Gryder himself shows up.

"Roz hurt Gryder terribly when she went back to her husband. After all, that piano player was an egomaniac. He thought he was the best pianist in the world. And the best lover. And the best writer—or whatever. But as much as I detested him, I know he loved Roz, too. He was obsessed with getting her back full-time, so he decided to write a book about the quartet and use it as a kind of blackmail on Ben.

"He began to hint to Roz that he'd found out a lot of strange things about everyone connected to the quartet. She reported it to Ben. Ben got more and more worried, afraid Gryder knew that he, Ben, had been a procurer. Ben knew that if Roz ever found out about his past, she'd leave him immediately. Can you imagine being married to the man who had orchestrated your own degradation, placed you in that kind of horror? No, of course not.

"Finally, Gryder came out and told Ben he was going to write this terrible book that told everything. Ben tried to talk him out of it. He tried everything—offering money, bankrolling tours and recordings for Will, anything. But Gryder refused. He wanted Roz or nothing.

"And finally that terrible night came when Ben stopped begging, stopped trying. And killed him. I saw him—afterward. He told me what had happened, and said he tried the best he could to make it look like a robbery gone sour. He gave me all Gryder's possessions to destroy. And I did—except for that ring."

"Did Ben arrange that car accident?" I asked.

"Yes. He told me he paid a kid from town to rig something up with a rope and a stuffed animal—I don't know who. He wanted to make it look as if the person who killed Gryder was out to get him, too. He was desperate. He even cooked up a story about me seeing Will beat up on him. He thought that if worse came to worse and he was charged with the killing, that might show that Will had been violent with him. It might point to self-defense."

Mrs. Wallace dropped the empty coffee container to the floor and stared down at it. "But he couldn't find the manuscript for the book," she muttered. "He searched and searched but he couldn't find it. And neither could I—not then, and not tonight."

"Roz has been in Seattle for days now playing with a group there. I was there looking after Ben in the apartment when the mail arrived the other day. We figured someone else was going to blackmail him. The card seemed to say that the manuscript was still here in the house. So we decided I should be the one to come up and look."

Donaldson spoke for the first time since we'd come inside: "Why does this man Polikoff have such a hold on you? Why did you go on helping him?"

She began to cry again, but soon she caught herself and wiped back the tears with her cap. "I've told you what Ben was once—a pimp. But

I didn't tell you that I was once also in the life. Yes, I was a whore. I was no longer young and I wanted out. Ben had a sick father at the time. He hired me to take care of the old man. He gave me a place to live, money, food, sent me to school, everything. And when the old man wanted to marry me, Ben gave us his blessings. No, it wasn't much of a marriage—his father was old and frail. But he actually loved me. Ben Polikoff gave me the chance to know what that can be like—to have someone truly love you. I'd do anything for him. And why not? He's paid his dues for the things he did when he was younger. Now he does nothing but look out for everyone else."

Ford Donaldson nodded to me then, seemingly acknowledging that we had all had enough for the moment. "I'm going to take Mrs. Wallace in now, Alice. We'll contact the NYPD about Polikoff. Why don't you and your friend go and get some rest? Just slam the door closed here, and I'll speak to you in the morning."

Holding her firmly by the arm, Donaldson led Mrs. Wallace toward the door.

"Just a second," I said. "Mrs. Wallace, did Ben have anything to do with the thefts of the kittens?"

She stared at me blankly.

"The Scottish Folds that were taken and sold," I said.

"I don't know what you're talking about," she said, confused. "Ben doesn't even like cats."

Tony and I walked back to the car. We were cold and depleted, but rather giddy with triumph.

Once inside, Tony said, "Let's play one quick

hand of casino. Eleven points. Loser buys drinks."

"Drinks! This isn't Manhattan, Tony. We're not going to find any place open for drinks."

"Don't worry about it. If I win, I have some other stakes in mind, anyway," he said mischievously.

"Besides," I protested, "you cheat!"

"Not me. It's you who was cheating. You don't even know the damn rules."

"All right, sucker," I said. "Deal."

"Great," he said, grinning. "And I bet you thought we were too old to neck in a car."

I started to win big. It was obvious that I was going to crush him. I already had three aces, the good ten, and most of the spades.

Tony began to chuckle. Which was unnerving, because he was being roundly beaten.

"I don't see anything funny about your situation, Basillio. You're going to have to finance the celebration."

"True. I wasn't laughing about that. I was laughing about how I had to drive all the way up to a backwash of the great state of Massachusetts to see the great Nestleton stymied."

"What do you mean 'stymied,' Basillio? I found out what happened, didn't I? My trap worked, didn't it? We know who the murderer is, don't we?"

"Yeah, Cat Lady, but it wasn't a feline crime. Your theory about the Scottish Fold thefts turns out to be meaningless. Mrs. Wallace didn't know what the hell you were talking about."

"Play the game, Tony," I said, slamming a card onto the seat. I beat him ten to one.

* * *

As we drove in and out of the sleeping town, looking for a pub, I thought of what Tony had said about my feline error. Maybe he was right, but Tony didn't know that Will Gryder had given Lulu to Beth Stimson. Why would he make a gift of that particular breed of kitten? Maybe because, many years before, he had cared for Scottish Fold kittens, after he'd stolen them along with their pedigree papers. But that was another crime. And Will Gryder was dead.

Of course we never found an open pub. So we went back to the hotel. I demanded the cash equivalent of four brandies from Basillio. He turned his pockets inside-out to show that he had no cash.

"Pretty low of you to welsh on a debt this way, Tony," I said, knowing there were three twenties in his other pants.

He outlined what those "other stakes" would entail, and I reluctantly agreed to the new terms of the pay-off. I figured that, on the whole, justice was being done.

**Be sure to catch the next
Alice Nestleton mystery,
Cat In a Glass House,
coming to you in
November 1993**

1

I was holding big, beautiful Bushy straight out over the sofa; his luxurious Maine Coon cat tail curled apprehensively beneath him, and his big eyes stared at me suspiciously.

"Bushy, I think I am going to become a movie star. How do you like those sardines?"

He squirmed out of my grasp and vaulted lightly to the carpet. Then, tail high, he strode away, his feelings ruffled. Well, Bushy was a skeptical cat. I was skeptical too, but something *was* happening.

Early that same morning I had received a phone call from my agent. She told me that a man named Brian Watts wanted to know if I was interested in doing a film. It was an Anglo-French production, to be shot in Malta (yes, Malta, which I really couldn't place geographically). The director was French —Claude Braque—whom I had heard of. And the film was a political thriller about the IRA and British Intelligence. My character would be an evil, Garbo-esque CIA operative.

"Be gentle with him," my agent had said before hanging up. "The pay is very good." She sounded as if I were some kind of demented cat-sitter who couldn't be trusted in social interactions with movie people.

At noon Brian Watts called. He was in Toronto and he would be arriving at Kennedy Airport around seven in the evening. Could he meet me at some restaurant downtown, around eight? Perhaps Dan Wu's, the new vegetarian Chinese restaurant in Tribeca? Oh course, I said. Delighted, I said. And I surely was. Dan Wu's was a gastronomic jewel. So I had read. And I had also read that a single meal there cost enough to pay half my rent. But Brian Watts was picking up the check. Yes, I was delighted.

After all, Dan Wu was the author of *Five Flavors*, one of the best Chinese cookbooks ever written, and I had purchased it three years ago. I had tried only one recipe, though—ginger duck. Disastrously.

So, while Bushy was skeptical, it really didn't hurt my feelings. I was already thinking of the dinner ahead.

I spent a few hours daydreaming about what I would do with the enormous sums of money that would be coming to me for my rather belated screen debut ... and whether or not I would choose to appear at the Oscar ceremony when I was nominated for Best Supporting Actress.

At six in the evening I had to make my dress decision. What does a forty-one-year-old stage actress qua cat-sitter wear to be courted, cinematically, in a posh Tribeca restaurant? Well, it was Tribeca, so I had to be a bit déclassé in order to be hip. And, since it was obviously a big-role-big-money part, I also had to be a bit elegant. So I chose an ankle-length, vampish dress, rose colored. Over it I wore a beat-up, short black denim jacket that had been given to me as a joke by my friend Basillio. No earrings. Long, yellow-gray hair worn loose.

I arrived at Dan Wu's on time, at eight. And Brian Watts was waiting for me in front of the restaurant. My heart sank when I saw him in the light reflected from the restaurant front. He was too old to be wearing the designer jeans he had on. He was too out of shape to be wearing the very hi-tech running shoes on his feet. And he was too agitated in manner to be wearing the very expensive and quite beautiful gray-on-gray silk sports jacket which seemed to have been crumpled with care to give that "laid-back" look.

Despite his British accent, he was obviously very "Hollywood," and the moment we stepped through the door together, he started a monologue, a kind of name-dropping babble about Bobbie and Swifty and Larry. None of whom meant a thing to me, but all of whom obviously meant a lot to Mr. Watts.

The restaurant was breathtaking. The main dining room was circular. The walls were white and unadorned. The round tables were all glass. The chairs were glass with black seats and back cushions. All the tableware was glass except for the chopsticks and other utensils, which were elegantly carved black wood.

The waitresses were beautiful, young Chinese women, all dressed in any way they wanted.

In the center of the dining room was the

kitchen—as if it had sprung out of the floor full blown, totally open in dazzling stainless steel. Wherever one sat in the room, one could see every step in the food preparation.

Four doors led out of the circle to the bathrooms and the cloakroom and the place where the dirty dishes were washed.

The multipage, totally vegetarian menu sent me into a kind of rapture. I wasn't familiar with a single dish. Oh, I recognized many of the ingredients, but not the dishes per se. For example, I knew both soy sauce and ginger but I had absolutely no idea what "soy-marinated shredded ginger" would look like or taste like. It was giddy reading. After all, I love Chinese food. The single most wonderful thing about New York when I first arrived in the city was the ready availability of all kinds of Chinese food. For a farm girl, it was a revelation. And now, more than twenty years later, I was a farm girl again, because this was a whole new Chinese cuisine to me.

Brian Watts started to talk about a dinner he had had in a Chinese restaurant somewhere south of Los Angeles with Sue and Denny. It was obvious he thought I knew who they were. I didn't. I smiled at him and returned to the menu. In my business, no one ever gets to the point until the dessert.

I read the menu as if it were a novel. Brian Watts kept up his monologue. From time to time I looked up from the menu and stared at him. He had a handsome face, just a bit bloated. His gaze kept roving over the room as he spoke, as if searching for friends. I felt neither affection nor enmity toward him. We were perfectly comfortable with each other. It was not real and neither of us minded.

Finally I made my selection.

First I would have "Sweet Peanut Soup with Strawberries."

Then I would have "Shredded Bean Curd with Golden Needles, Mushrooms, Wood Ears and Eggs."

Just giving the order to the waitress was exciting. Of course, I had absolutely no idea what "Golden Needles" were.

Then Brian Watts, for the first time, looked at me long and hard and a trifle critically. And I realized that he was looking at me in that weird kind of way that "sophisticated" men often use with women they don't approve of.

"What you ordered," he noted, "is just a kind of vegetarian Mu Shou Rou." Since I didn't know what Mu Shou Rou was, there was nothing I could say.

I smiled. He started to talk again. I felt more friendly toward him. My eyes moved toward that stainless-steel island of a kitchen where white garbed geniuses were creating remarkable tastes. I saw pots and flames and woks and knives being manipulated, but heard few sounds.

Then I saw the cat. An enormous red tabby was napping like a rag doll on the ledge of one of the stainless-steel shelves, up high.

The only parts of the tabby moving were the tail and one twitching paw. What a wonderful place to snooze, I thought. What a beautiful kitchen cat, I also thought.

Yes, Dan Wu's was a spectacular dining spot. No doubt about that.

Our waitress appeared and placed a glass carafe of hot tea and two small glasses on the table.

Brian Watts expertly picked up the carafe by its long neck and started to pour tea into my cup. For a moment I panicked. Hadn't Brian Watts had a grandmother who warned him never, never, never to pour hot tea into a glass without first placing a spoon in the glass so that it does not shatter? He obviously hadn't. But it didn't matter. The glass did not break.

I sat back, relieved. Brian and I smiled at each other.

I looked back at the high kitchen shelves. Red Tabby had awakened and was surveying the customers, counting the house. What a beautiful cat!

Suddenly my eyes filled with tears. I blinked them away. The red tabby had brought back to me a wonderful memory from my childhood of watching my grandmother rock herself to sleep on her chair with Henrietta on her lap. Grandma had "inside" cats and "outside" cats—barn cats and house cats—but she had only one lap cat: a big old red tabby named Henrietta.

I had this wonderful desire to rush to the shelf and grab Red Tabby. Then I would bring her back to the table and rock her in my lap just like Grandma used to rock Henrietta. But I didn't move.

Red Tabby knew what I was thinking, though. I could sense it.

I smiled again at Brian Watts to let him know I was back on his wavelength.

"You did some rep work in Montreal, didn't you?" He asked. There was no doubt about it—he had a very handsome face. He looked just a bit like Terrence Stamp.

"Yes, I did. Some Shakespeare."

"Then we probably know the same people up there," he noted.

I didn't answer. At that moment, something very strange was happening.

The restaurant became absolutely still. There hadn't been much noise, anyway—just the usual low hum and the sounds from the stainless steel kitchen island. But even those muted sounds had stopped. I mean the place was mute.

I looked at Brian Watts. He was staring past me and his face had grown pale.

I turned in my chair to follow his gaze.

Three young men were standing casually, side by side, about ten feet into the main room. They were Chinese. They were handsome and well dressed. They seemed very young, almost teenagers. Their jackets were much too large for them, and too long. They wore shirts and ties.

Each carried a small, ugly, blackish object in his hands, cradling the object gently as if it were a bird.

Then one of them detached himself from the group and walked to a wall. He removed a can of spray paint from his jacket pocket and began to draw a single large Chinese character in red paint on the brilliantly white wall.

The hostess came out of the stainless-steel kitchen, walking toward the graffiti artist. She walked slowly, obviously frightened and confused. She was speaking to him in a low voice in Chinese.

The artist flung the spray can at her, striking

her on the neck. The hostess staggered backward.

Someone in the restaurant screamed.

Then the shooting started. Brian Watts threw himself on the floor. I did the same.

It wasn't like in the movies. The firing somehow sounded distant. Dull, staccato bass grunts. It was the results that brought the terror. The bullets chewed up walls and glass splintered everywhere. I was so frightened my fingernails dug into my palms and drew blood.

Then there was silence again. Slowly, people began getting up and looking around, but there was little to see because it was dark. The three young men had vanished. Brian Watts helped me up.

The lights had been shattered. Then someone opened the doors which led out of the main dining area so that light could filter in.

Ten feet away from our table lay our waitress, her right leg and right arm stretched out. Her long black hair, which had been tied up, now wreathed her face. Her hair was speckled with a pattern of blood. Her face had a look of absolute repose. Her eyes were wide open. She was obviously dead. I started to cry. I tried to get to her, but my limbs were no longer taking commands. Brian Watts was trying to light a cigarette. I began to shake. And then the strangest thought came into my head: That I would never, as long as I lived, taste Sweet Peanut Soup with Strawberries.